I0734340

Conversations With the Moon

Amy Neftzger

Fields of Gold
Publishing, Inc.

Published by
Fog Ink

Fog Ink
PO Box 128438
Nashville TN, 37212

Edited by Ken McManus

ISBN: 978-1-940894-28-7

For T.N., who explained to
me why the moon is a tenor.

Conjectures on the Moon

Ivory moon
With a curious stare
Thinking of earth
And what you'd find there

Reflection glows
In alabaster eyes
Your musing rays
Pierce through the miles

Mysterious
You think of your neighbor
Beams reach and tousle
Churning white vapors

Colorful things
Borrowed light will explore
Circling in search
Of mortals and more

Dreaming of blue
And the substance contained
Watching it flow
Wishing it explained

Gaze upon land
So far from your own kind
Touch it with light
And make it sublime

Wonder away
Inimitable friend
Conjecture also
Reigns down on this end

Table of Contents

Prologue
A Few Preliminary Remarks

The moon is an intimate friend of mine. We talk almost every night. He knows just about everything there is to know about me, but I am a simple creature. The moon, however, is more complex and given to many moods and phases. He changes his disposition from one night to the next.

My friend is much older than I am. He's seen more of life than I have. He's also seen more of death. He's been a witness to countless loves and wars in every language; he speaks them all. He has experienced things throughout his time that I have never dreamed. In fact, he has given many of us our dreams. We think that we conceive them on our own, but the moon plants the seeds of dreams within the heart. He can be quite mischievous in this manner at times, as you shall see.

He's a very curious thing. He sees everything that happens on earth, but he doesn't always understand. He isn't human. He's seen all there is to observe but has experienced little. This makes him all the more curious. He has just as many questions as answers for me, and some nights we talk until dawn. He surprises me constantly.

The moon is a passionate, unpredictable creature given to many moods. But regardless of his nightly humor, he always has a story. Here are a few that he has told me.

Chapter
One

In the Proximity of Moonlight

The moon is particularly bright this evening. He seems to be smiling at some great satisfaction. I can see him clearly through the silhouette of the barren trees. I look up at him through a cloud of my own frosty breath as I remark aloud that it's a fine evening. I watch the puffs of frosty breath disappear, and then I hear him speak for the first time.

"The evening is too fine and my light too magnificent for anyone to spend this time alone." His silvery voice shimmers down to my ears.

I first turn around to look behind me, although I had clearly heard the voice coming from above. "You are not deceived." He smiles kindly at me. "It is I, the moon."

His voice is like liquid poetry flowing through me. The sound doesn't stop when it reaches my ears; it continues to resonate through my entire body.

"How is it that you can speak?" Now that I know him better, the question seems foolish. But at the time I was dumbfounded and didn't know what else to say. After all, what does any mortal say to the moon upon first conversing?

"I speak when I choose and to whom I choose. No one can hear me speaking, except for those I wish to be my audience." This is part of his magic. If there were anyone standing nearby to whom the moon wishes to remain anonymous, the person would fail to hear the moon's voice or to even see his face. The moon would appear as nothing more than a stoic mass of illuminated stone in the night sky.

"Do you speak to many people?"

"A few," he remarks with an air of pretension that tells me more than his words. He chooses his audience carefully. "I speak every language -- even those of the stars, the animals, and the trees. But I wouldn't advise talking with the trees this time of year. Every autumn they fall into the depths of despair and insist that their leaves will never return. They're quite dramatic about it all. Of course, the leaves return in the spring, but there's no use explaining that to a melancholy poplar. I simply don't bother with them." After giving me this off-hand advice, his tone becomes playful. "I have watched you for some time."

"I have watched you, as well. But I never dreamed that you were capable of watching me."

"It makes me by far the better observer." He smiles knowingly at this thought. What things might he have seen? What knowledge he must have! His smile conveys it all in a single moment.

"What have you seen that might interest me?" I inquire with anticipation. He is fanciful and content, all at the same time. Clearly, he's pleased that I'm so interested in him. The sparkle in his eyes becomes more spirited as he prepares his answer.

"In one night, I see enough interesting events to last a human lifetime. But the most fascinating of all these things are the effects that individuals have on one another. Perhaps this is the essence of life: that it is not entirely independent." He closes his eyes in a thoughtful manner. As he raises his eyelids, moonbeams splatter shimmering rays from his eyelashes and fan out across the galaxy. "Take you and me, for instance," he continues.

"Two entities cannot exist without influencing each other. Even if the two beings never acknowledge each other, the mere proximity of one will have an effect on the other."

"But how close must two entities exist before their effect upon each other is made known?"

"Proximity is relative. You and I are far apart, yet we influence each other nightly. When I look down at earth, I see that proximity is never farther than my moonbeams can reach, and that is nearly everywhere. You only have to be on the same planet to have your life affect another life." He pauses. I think this was for effect, rather than to collect his thoughts. "The earth is a good example. There are many people who seek isolation, but it is impossible. It cannot be. Mere existence requires interaction. It is inevitable." He pauses to sigh. I admire his incandescent stream of breath as it rushes through the heavens, dancing a meandering path through the starry night. His breath moves more like an illuminated ballerina twirling across a stage than a wind through space. It glows brilliantly. "I am reminded of a story." And here he began his first narration of many.

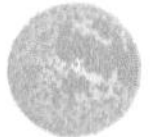

It was after midnight when Sydney turned slowly onto Main Street. She recalled walking this same route with her father when she was 10 years old. The image imbedded in her mind was of how she had vigorously tugged at her father's hand as they leisurely strolled together. Perhaps it's better said that Michael, Sydney's father, strolled. Sydney was more of a bouncer. She skipped and hopped with exuberance while asking question upon question about everything she saw. She'd been down Main Street hundreds of times before, but she was a curious thing by nature and always had new inquiries. Maybe that's why she'd left Samsonville as soon as she turned nineteen. She simply wanted to know what else was out there.

"How do you know there really is an 'out there'?" her father had asked when Sydney announced that she was going out into the world. He glanced over the cut-out pattern pieces scattered across the dining room table, where his wife had been sewing herself a new dress. He picked up the bright red pincushion and gently tapped his fingers on the mosaic of pinheads stuck into the facing. "Maybe every other place is just like this one."

"They couldn't all be," Sydney insisted with faint disgust, pulling her shiny black mane into a ponytail at the base of her neck. She held the hair loosely in place with one hand as her mouth turned into a half frown. "That'd be such a disappointment that I simply can't believe it could be true."

"Well, now, there's an interesting yardstick for measuring truth." Michael picked up a worn-out tape measure and dangled the flimsy ruler to the floor as he spoke. Sydney thought he was talking about the sewing instrument, and so she deliberately pulled her mouth into a complete frown. Then she released her hair with a dramatic flick of her wrist, quickly turned on her heel, and left the room. Later the following day she left town.

Quite some time had passed since then. Sydney was much older now and her father had just passed away, though one couldn't really say that he'd left. He would be buried in the town cemetery in two days. Not even death would release him from Samsonville. The small town had a strong hold on most of its occupants. Even Sydney's mother, Karen, refused to come to live in New York with Sydney, but Sydney hoped to change her mother's mind after the funeral. Sydney had two months of vacation, and when she received the news of her father's death, she decided to take it all at once to be with her mother.

Tonight Sydney drove meticulously. She stopped at each corner, even though she knew that no one else would be on the street. Not even the sheriff would be awake at this hour. He was only a part-time sheriff, anyway, and the people of Samsonville were courteous enough to schedule their crimes and misdemeanors for those three afternoons a week when the law was on-duty.

Sydney could almost hear the occupants snoring in unison. Underneath her stylish pants, her legs ached from the long drive. Even when traveling, Sydney dressed well. When she was still a girl, her mother taught her how to be fashionable on a budget. Now that she was in her thirties Sydney could not dress sloppily, even when she tried.

Sydney turned into the drive of her parents' house and listened to the familiar creaking of the gravel beneath her tires. She thought about how everyone would know that she'd come home. This was one of the things Sydney didn't like about small towns. There's no way to keep a secret when everyone knows everyone else. Sydney liked her privacy and she didn't feel like making small talk with anyone she hadn't seen for a few years.

Sydney and her mother grieved deeply during the funeral. Most of the town did, also. Michael was well respected, and even those who weren't close to the family attended the funeral, since it was as much of a social event as the town would see for several months. The entire day was a blur of faces in black. Sydney politely endured small talk with hundreds of people she scarcely remembered, but the entire time she wished she could be alone with Karen and simply cry. When the day was over and she was alone with her mother, Sydney finally felt the freedom to grieve without any restraint.

For two weeks after the funeral, she managed to stay indoors and away from crowds. Sydney had a goal: she'd come to help her mother and not to renew old acquain-.

tances.

It wasn't that Sydney had anything against the locals. She simply disliked being the object of conversation. She'd left the small-town atmosphere for the anonymity and excitement of the larger city. During her stay Sydney was content to keep house and tend to her mother's needs. But one morning Karen decided that her daughter was growing restless, and she made an unusual request.

"Sydney," Karen put down the newspaper she was reading and waited for Sydney to look up. "Sydney, I want you to go down to the City Café and have breakfast this morning."

"I don't eat breakfast." Sydney buried her head back in her magazine.

"You don't have to eat. Just have coffee." Karen waited for Sydney to look up again, but Sydney continued her pretense of reading. "That's where everyone goes for breakfast. If there's any news, they'll be talking about it down there."

"There's nothing new. This town hasn't changed in twenty years."

"News is relative. Nothing seems new to you because

you're used to the sensational headlines of bigger cities."

Sydney thought briefly about the City Café. She'd never eaten the food there. When she was a teenager, she swore that she'd rather die than get a life sentence warming the vinyl chairs in the café. It was the central meeting place for the townspeople. But to a teenager, it was the end of the road; like a neon sign announcing that you had become nothing of importance. Teenagers thought adults went to the City Café because they couldn't go anywhere else in life.

"It's all small talk." Sydney finally looked up. "I hate that. They sit around for hours every morning, talking about the same things. What do you want me to go there for?"

"Well," Karen paused, "Your father used to go there at least once a week. I just thought that some of his friends might be wondering how I'm doing. If you went there, you could tell them."

"Mom, I don't want to go."

"Please, Sydney."

Sydney let out a slow breath and then stood up. She

couldn't resist her mother's plea.

"You want me to bring you anything?"

"Just the news." Karen didn't smile, but she might as well have.

When Sydney reached the glass front of the City Café, she pretended to stare at the menu posted by the door as she stole glances inside at the patrons. She tried to recognize the faces, but although they looked familiar, she couldn't recall names. She had just seen many of these people at Michael's funeral, but she was busy putting on a brave front and hadn't paid attention to the conversations much. She couldn't remember much of what anyone said to her at the funeral or who was present.

What she did remember clearly was the first and last time she went into the City Café. It was over fifteen years ago. She was still a teenager and went in on a dare. Sydney and her friends were young enough to believe that they would never be one of those people sitting at the tables and going nowhere. She'd once mocked the patrons of the café and branded them as stiffs who occupied "vinyl coffins." It was Sydney who coined the phrase "doomed to Formica," which referred to anyone who never ventured beyond the city limits. On the morning of the dare, Sydney and a group of practical jokers brought a dozen frogs into the café and ordered breakfast for the amphibians. Maybe this wouldn't have been so bad if the frogs hadn't been packed in jars of formaldehyde.

Sydney continued her pretense of reading the menu for quite some time. Many of the faces she saw were the very people who'd sat in the same chairs years ago. They were simply older. Then the door of the café opened partially, and a tall figured leaned in the doorway. Sydney ignored the man until she heard his voice.

"It doesn't smell like formaldehyde in here." Sydney glanced nervously at him and then looked away. He smiled knowingly at her, but Sydney couldn't remember him. She'd spoken with too many forgotten acquaintances at the funeral to know if she'd seen him there.

"It wasn't that," Sydney responded defensively. She slipped the strap of her designer purse from her shoulder and held the bag loosely at her side.

"Sure it was." He stepped completely outside and leaned against the glass front of the building. "You used to say that the only way anyone would get you inside this place was if they pumped formaldehyde into your veins first. That's how we came up with the idea of the frogs."

"I did say that, didn't I?" Sydney stared absent-mindedly into his deep brown eyes. Snippets of memories passed through her head before finally converging into a solid picture. She remembered going to high school with him. He was president of the student government then. Maybe he was a politician now. His wardrobe looked as if it came straight from an Eddie Bauer catalog.

"I said the same thing once, too," he confessed. He looked at her expectantly, but she was still too busy trying to remember his name to make conversation. After a few moments of silence he stood erectly. "Well," he started hesitantly, then glanced across the street and waved at someone Sydney couldn't see. "I have a bet that you're a big enough person to come inside the door. Mike Smee doesn't think you have the guts to set foot in this place after the frog party." Sydney smiled at the recollection, and with the mention of Mike's name she knew this was Brian Wellman.

"I forgot you two were there. Does Bonnie still own this place?"

"Sure."

Sydney pretended to look at the menu again. She sighed deeply to herself and stepped around Brian before opening the door and walking inside. She knew everyone was looking at her. She even heard several people whisper her name. Bonnie was standing at a table nearby, holding a coffee pot in one hand while the other rested on her hip. She looked the same. Twenty years had done nothing to age her.

"Just so you know," Bonnie said loud enough for the whole restaurant to hear, "That even though you didn't pay your bill the last time you was here that I'm not holdin' it against you. Them frogs didn't eat much at all."

"Thanks, Bonnie." Sydney wished she were still outside when Brian suddenly spoke up from behind her.

"Bonnie, you know those frogs were some of your best customers. You talked about how they didn't keep asking you for stuff every five minutes or leave a mess on the floor. You even said they tipped as well as your regular customers, even if it wasn't in cash. And you told everyone how those frogs treated you better than most of the people in this town. I think maybe you even dated one for a while."

"That wasn't a dead frog. That was Earl McCarter." Bonnie's tone was nearly always stoic, even when she made other people laugh.

Sydney quickly got over her embarrassment, and after that first visit she found herself going back to the café often. Brian filled her in on what she'd missed during her absence. It was more than she thought, or maybe it was the way Brian explained it all.

The café had a very casual atmosphere. It wasn't unusual for people at different tables to talk to one another. Sydney learned a lot this way. When Old Jensen complained about Matilda to someone across the way, Sydney remarked that she thought Jensen's wife was named Kim.

"Kim's his wife," Brian confirmed with a nod.

"Then who's Matilda?"

"His tractor. That's what he calls her when she's running well. Old Jensen has about thirty names for his tractor. When she purrs beautifully, he says that he's 'waltzing with Matilda.' When the engine gives him trouble, she's 'the old b---h,' and if it's just a little cold out and it doesn't start right up, he calls her 'the little mule.'"

Sydney laughed.

"The more nicknames you have for something, the more you love it. Old Jensen has more nicknames for his tractor than he has for his wife." Brian smiled softly to himself. "That tells you everything right there."

"How many nicknames did your parents have for you?"

"Three."

"Aren't you going to tell me what they are?"

"They're not flattering."

He eventually told her, anyway. He was glad he did when he saw her laugh. Her eyes seemed to be a clearer blue when she laughed, like the pure sound that a crystal glass makes when it rings.

It wasn't long before Sydney started coming to the café and actually eating breakfast there every morning. If she didn't overhear the day's news from someone else in the restaurant, Brian filled her in. The conversation didn't run out, even when there really wasn't any news.

"You know," she confessed one morning over her omelet, "I didn't want to come in here that first day because I thought it was pointless."

"What is?"

"Small talk. That's all people do here. They show up every day and say the same things they did the day before."

"Small talk leads to bigger things. It's like fishing: you need a little fish to catch the big fish."

"Nothing big ever happens here."

"What's big?" he asked. He put his fork down and waited for her to answer as he sipped a glass of orange juice. Sydney had to think. At first she wasn't sure what she meant by the word. Then she answered him.

"Things that affect the world." He put the glass of juice down on the table.

"Well, that's where you're wrong."

"What happens in this town that affects the world?"

"This town is their world."

"Have you ever left this place and gone more than sixty miles from here? A vacation or something?"

"No."

"You've never thought about getting out of this town and going somewhere?"

"Where?"

"Anywhere."

"For what?"

"I don't know. Don't you ever want to go find yourself, or something?"

"Most people who go looking for themselves don't know what they've lost to begin with. While they're out searching for the treasures the world has to offer, they lose the ones inside of themselves. They don't find themselves; they lose who they were to begin with. They lose contact with the things that made them. They lose the things and relationships that were good for them."

Sydney shifted uneasily in her seat. Suddenly she felt like he knew more about the world than she did, and she'd seen more of it.

"Do you miss your job?" he asked suddenly. Sydney was glad for the change of subject.

"I'm on vacation, but I still work a little from my mother's house. I did miss the office and the city at first." She hesitated, as if she couldn't think clearly. "Now I don't miss anything except maybe some good Chinese food."

"Go to Creightonville. There's a Chinese restaurant on the square now."

"Do you have all the answers?" she asked with a

smile.

"Just the ones you need." He couldn't make the reply without laughing. Like most things about him, his laugh was quiet and sincere. Sydney was quickly laughing with him. For the first time it felt good to be home.

The next morning she sat down across from him and quickly asked, "What's new today, Answer Man?" His expression was serious.

"Mrs. Walker finally put that old dog to sleep."

"Barney?"

"That's the one."

"That dog must have been very old. She's had him for a number of years."

"Twenty-two." He paused when Bonnie arrived to take their order. He almost always ordered the same thing. Sydney decided that today would be different.

"Live a little. Get those eggs fried," she insisted.

"I like them scrambled."

"Then order bacon. Every day you order the same thing because it's comfortable. It's the same reason that every man in this town marries his high school sweetheart: because it's comfortable. Where's your spirit of adventure?"

"I didn't marry my high school sweetheart," he in-sisted. "She married a dentist." Sydney brushed the comment aside and turned to Bonnie.

"Bonnie, we'd like something different. Bring us whatever you think is the best you've got today."

"Sure thing," Bonnie replied, nodding, and headed for the kitchen.

"Just make sure there's coffee," Brian added before Bonnie had traveled too far. He looked at Sydney with concern. "I'm not so sure she gave all those frogs back to the school. What if she serves us a couple of stale amphibians on toast?"

"I wouldn't put it past her. But what about Barney? Mrs. Walker swore she wouldn't ever put him to sleep."

"Well, she finally did. The last time I saw him, he was completely bald. She was walking him near the park. A stray cat walked right up to him, like the cat knew Barney was too old to do anything about it. Barney would just sort of tremble, like he was really angry. It took a lot out of him just to work up a decent bark. So Mrs. Walker smacked that stupid cat on his head with her cane and cussed him out. Everybody heard her."

"Learn any new words?"

"I teach him new words all the time," Bonnie re-marked as she arrived at the table. She quickly poured the coffee and delivered two ham omelets. Then she scurried off to other tables.

"I learned how many cuss words old Mrs. Walker knew, that's for sure." Brian continued. "She never talked like that when she was our Sunday school teacher." His smile was gentle, lacking in judgment or condemnation. Suddenly he dropped the smile and cocked his head a lit-tle, as if he was carefully unfolding something fragile in-side of himself. "He was a good dog. But everyone knew that he'd outlived his time except Mrs. Walker. Even the squirrels used to sit on the window sill and make faces at Barney until he barked."

"I hope nobody ever keeps me around past my time." Sydney remarked off-handedly as she cut into the omelet. Brian leaned back and studied her. Sydney paused in mid-action to stare back into his tanned face. He put one elbow over the back of the vinyl seat.

"You think you can control that?" he asked quietly.

"I can try." She sat up a little straighter and pulled her coffee cup to her lips. She peered over the top defiantly. "I think that when it's over it's over." She slowly sipped from the cup and stared him down from behind the rim of the mug.

"Sure," he replied back in that casual manner of his. "But you're not the umpire. We all have to play until the game's over. When it's up, it's up. But we play until the last out is called." Sydney put the coffee cup down firmly on the table.

"There are times when you know the game is over just by looking at the score."

"You still play it out to the end." He was talking with one of his hands again. The motion was graceful, yet rhythmic. It distracted her. "Otherwise," he continued, "the other team wins by forfeit, and that's not really winning. Even if you're just going through the motions, you play to the end or you're not really playing fairly, are you?"

"Life isn't a game." She was smiling, but something in her clear blue eyes made him uneasy. She appeared a bit paler than usual.

"I didn't say that it was." He put both of his hands

down on the table. "It was only a metaphor."

"I don't care for sports."

"You don't have to, Sydney." His voice was soft but not apologetic. "It's okay not to like things. That's what makes everyone different: we don't all like the same things. And I think this town would be a boring place if we were all exactly alike." He tried to look in her eyes, but she was staring down at the gold flecks in the Formica table. "It's okay not to like death, or not to like that part of life that leads to it. That's the hardest part of life, I think. But for some reason most of us have to live through it."

"I'm not thinking about my father. Or my mother."

"You're not thinking about how she's taking her situation, but you're thinking about how hard it would be for you if you were in her shoes." There was a very long silence. There was no awkwardness to the lack of conversation, but a thoughtfulness that Sydney found unfamiliar. Sydney listened to the echoes of conversations from other tables and then suddenly shook her head.

"I don't know what I'm thinking. I'm not even sure what I'm feeling. Why are we always talking about death, anyway?"

"It's part of life." Brian's shoulders came up into a slight shrug and then dropped again as he said this, as if such conversations were commonplace. Perhaps they were.

"I think I'd just rather talk about something else this morning." She was now less talkative than usual, but not because she didn't feel like talking. The content of the conversation didn't really bother Sydney, but there was something more. She'd suddenly realized that she never talked to her other friends about these things. It wasn't as if New Yorkers or other city dwellers were shallow people, but it occurred to Sydney that she never talked to anyone else about deeper issues the way she talked to Brian. She'd traveled the whole world, looking for something extraordinary. It was surprising to her that she found it here, and it scared her a little. She went home and repeated the day's news to her mother.

"Thank God," was the only reply Karen made when she heard about Barney.

A week later Sydney's boss offered her an assignment overseas. Sydney asked for a few days to think it over, but she didn't wait for the next morning before talking with

Brian. She drove to his farm to look for him. The roads hadn't changed, but Sydney's recollection had. She got lost on the way, but after back-tracking down a few wrong turns, she finally arrived.

It was late afternoon and his car was there, but Sydney couldn't easily find him. She rang the doorbell. No answer. Then she started searching the grounds. Everything was in order and neatly arranged. For a man who worked with dirt, he was incredibly tidy. She was about to walk into the barn when she spotted him sitting on a fence, gazing thoughtfully over a field of corn. His back was to her. She walked slowly out toward him, calling his name when she came near. He jumped off the fence and turned around. Sydney watched the rays of afternoon sun glisten on the edge of his blonde hair as he started toward her. She glanced over the cornfield behind his silhouette. The amber rays of fiery afternoon sun made the stalks appear as shining gold spears. The wind gently parted the neat rows, making the corn look like soldiers bowing in succession.

"The color is so yellow this time of day. They look like treasure," Sydney remarked with admiration when he had drawn nearer.

"Well, they're not real gold. But it brings in money, so I don't think it's fools gold." He looked her over. She was stylishly dressed, as usual. "You didn't come here to play in the cornfield, did you?"

"No, but now I wish I had. It's beautiful this time of day." She glanced over the view again. Then she told him why she was there. He listened patiently with both of his hands in his pockets. She paused several times, as if waiting for him to say something. But he simply listened. When she finished telling him the details of the assignment, he took his hands out of his pockets and folded his arms.

"You're always looking for someplace to go, Sydney. It sounds like something you'd like."

"You never think about leaving?"

"I can't find a reason to leave. Everything I need is here right now." He paused for a moment to look back at his house. "You can't find a reason to stay. You think everything you need is out there someplace." He nodded in the direction of the sun as he spoke.

"Not everything." She answered him so quickly that the speed of the reply surprised them both. He glanced thoughtfully back at the cornfield. He squinted directly at the sun for a moment, wondering if the moment would set also. Then his eyes came to rest upon her again. He drew in a long breath, then gave the moment to silence and took her hand without speaking. Sydney stared out at the cornfield again. The amber light of late afternoon sun was playfully christening each stalk, kissing the golden soldiers goodbye before the long journey into the west. Sydney put her head on Brian's shoulder as they watched the sun vanish and fade behind the tall rows of vegetation.

"Let the sun go where it will," she thought. She felt no urge to follow it. For now she was content to stay just where she was.

"Sydney spent much of her life seeking isolation and avoiding her hometown in search of bigger things. She was certain that the only way to discover happiness, success, or understanding was to go out looking for them," the moon explains. "She finally found the things she wanted most in the last place she wanted to look for them. But Sydney could not recognize fullness, meaning, happiness or greatness until she had seen the lack of these things."

I am silent as I begin to ponder how the moon sees everything so clearly with his light -- things that we often fail to see even when they're spread out before us like a feast. He pokes his chin forward and glances down at his beard. It is still in celestial order, and so he glances across the earth, scattering moonbeams across the continent as he does so. "How I wish you could see the Aurora Borealis tonight. It is remarkable."

"So are you, my friend." He smiles knowingly at my comment, but without any trace of condescension. Then he winks at me. The rays from his eye flood down upon me as his eye reopens, and I feel the light touching the deepest part of me.

Chapter
Two
A Doorway to the Moon

"You have many names," I remark one evening to my friend the moon.

"Yes," he agrees. "Many names and even more moods." He appears in a contemplative humor. He's often in this state. It's the frame of mind from which he forms most of his conjecture about the earth.

"Which name do you prefer?"

"Does it matter what one calls me?"

"Don't quote Shakespeare to me," I beg. "It's overdone."

"I didn't." He insists. But he's annoyed with me and his disdain tells me that he was about to do so. He is silent. I watch him exhale silvery rays of light that descend upon the earth with a gentle force.

"Your names. Which one do you prefer?"

"I prefer to be recognized for who I am, rather than what I'm called."

"But everyone likes to be called by a certain name," I persist. His ambivalence increases my desire for an answer. I begin walking casually down my driveway toward the street. The black asphalt ahead of me glistens with the moon's distorted reflection as I inhale the misty remains of an earlier downpour. As I gaze farther down the road, his light seems to travel with my eyes into the distance. "Can you see your reflection on the wet roads?" I ask as I admire the visual effect.

"I see my reflection everywhere: on the wet streets of every city, across the tops of the trees moist with dew, on the surface of every graceful wave in the oceans, in the stillness of every pond, in the shine of a well polished automobile, in the eyes of every lover, and in the heart of every poet."

"You're something of a poet yourself," I remark with admiration.

"A poet is anyone who has the ability to grasp the eternal within the ordinary; to see the extraordinary beauty in the everyday."

"That's you!" He's clearly pleased at my exclamation. Tonight his form is sleek and magnificently trim. His slip of a smile accentuates the outline of his crescent shape. Then his smile elongates momentarily as he chuckles. The moon dust in his breath sparkles more brilliantly when he laughs.

"Perhaps I am, at that!" He continues to chuckle forth bursts of brilliant celestial powder. I reach up to feel this glimmering dust brush against my outstretched arm, and his light bathes my skin. There is no light like moonlight. It is both coolness and warmth, and it reaches tenderly into the soul. Moonlight lacks the harshness of sunlight. Moonlight brings out the best in most of us. I am grateful to him for this, and he knows it.

"I wonder if there are many poets behind the closed doors of this city," I muse aloud as I glance at the neighboring houses.

"There are." He nods with a knowing air that somehow conveys a bit of remorse. "Some of these poets work behind closed doors, producing works of art that open the doors of eternity for others." As he pauses, I look up at the trees and wonder how his light appears as it is reflected back to him. Then I glance back at the nearby houses and wonder how much he knows of what goes on behind these closed doors. "Doors can be fascinating things. The ability of one individual to influence another is often a simple matter of opening a door or not opening a door. Fate rests upon just such a precipice. The doors encountered in life can lead one down a myriad of paths." He pauses to glance over the lights of the city. He isn't blinded by the electric lights. He can see just as well in darkness, daylight, or artificial light. Moonlight is a different substance. It has an enchantment about it that reaches beyond the ordinary and gives him insight into the deepest part of us.

"You bring up a good point," I remark with admiration. "I suppose I really think of doors only in terms of privacy."

"Doors can be elusive or tangible in nature." As he begins to smile warmly, his aura of light increases in brightness. "I am reminded of a story."

The grass is too wet to sit upon, and so I resume my wandering down the damp street as I gaze upward and wait for him to begin.

Every door signifies a point of passage. One has only to look at a door, and the mind wanders to the other side without provocation. Any door can beckon. Almost every door does so simply through a stoic appearance. In fact, the more solid a door appears to be, the more likely we are to wonder what treasure it might be protecting.

But doors are built for different purposes, and different doors lead to distinct and separate destinations. Doors can be physical, emotional, or spiritual. Walking through any door can change a life. Not walking through a door can cause just as much of an alteration. This is because every person's life is filled with doors, with people entering and exiting our lives at different times. It is the pattern of opening and closing doors that determines the path that anyone's life takes.

Doors are more than a simple part of life: doors are what make life what it is. Every door encountered forms the road of life. Jane and Molly knew this and recognized the importance of doors at an early age. Doors held a special significance for the two of them.

When they were still quite small, Jane and Molly played a game of opening and closing doors. Aunt Stacy would stand in the hallway and each child would take a turn quickly opening and slamming the door that she stood behind. Aunt Stacy would try to catch the door while it was open, as if she were trying to get out of the hallway. The girls laughed as they kept her a prisoner there. She was trapped in a point of passage, frozen in transition for the duration of the game. When it was time for them to leave, Molly shouted and screamed her goodbyes louder than anyone.

"There's no freight train, Little One. There's no need for you to use such a loud voice."

"Oh," Jane explained off-handedly, "Molly always likes to leave with a bang. That's how you know when she's gone."

"Noise to silence." Aunt Stacy nodded her understanding, but not her approval. "How dramatic."

It was theatrical, but that was Molly. She did everything largely.

This was their game of doors. They played the game every time they saw Aunt Stacy, which was often.

Sometimes the game lasted a few minutes. Other times the game lasted for more than an hour. The girls didn't think about why Aunt Stacy never won. They simply devised new strategies to keep Aunt Stacy locked in the hallway. Now that the girls are older, Aunt Stacy is no longer there to play with them. The girls know which door she finally passed through: it was the one that no human hand could hold closed.

Molly liked to think that Aunt Stacy felt the brush of angels' wings as she passed through that gilded doorway. The very thought of it would give Molly the most delightful goose bumps. Besides being theatrical, Molly was something of an expressionist and amateur poet. She wrote poems about her childhood games with Aunt Stacy, and she danced whenever she heard music, even if it was in the grocery store. In fact, this was how she met her first husband. Molly was in a shoe store, doing a soft ballet routine to the driving rhythm of an alternative rock piece. Dan walked through the neon lighted glass doorway when he saw her. He came into the store because he thought she was something else. Most people did, also. But Dan bought Molly the shoes she was dancing in and told her that they must be magical to cause such a beautiful sight. Dan was a poet, and Molly was more in love with Dan's words than with him.

"When you leave here, do you fly up to heaven and dance among the other stars at night?" was the first question he asked of her.

"Watch and see," Molly replied with a confident demeanor, as she continued to dance.

"If I get too close to you then, will I get burned? Or are you a friendly light?"

"There's only one way to find out. Do you believe in risks? Or are you more in love with words than life?"

"Of course I love words more than life. I'm a writer. Actually, I'm a poet." This was all he needed to say for Molly to fall in love. During the entire time they were together, Molly cared more about what he wrote than what he did with his life. Dan was telling the absolute truth: he was far more careful with his words than with his life. In fact, his lifestyle was somewhat reckless, and eventually he and Molly divorced. He wrote sonnets about his relationship with Molly and published them as a book. She was flattered, even though the book was less than complimen tary toward Molly at the end.

"Part of life," she exclaimed with a careless attitude. "You can't expect an ex-husband to write good things about his former wife. He might regret the divorce then, and I wouldn't want him to do that. We're better off. So let him hate me."

While Jane stayed cautious and single, Molly tried on husbands as if they were new clothes. Some of them weren't even her own. She was married and divorced four times by the age of thirty-five. She was almost always involved with someone.

Despite their different personalities, the sisters had always been close. Their whole lives they discussed their choices openly with each other. If one had a job opportunity, she would always call the other and they would meet at Jane's house, in the study behind the paned glass doors. This was the room where they did their most serious talking. It was in this room lined with paperback books that Jane first told Molly about Sammy.

Like her name implies, Jane was the more sensible of the two sisters. Rarely did she give over to her passions, and yet she indulged in Sammy. Perhaps it was the way they met. Jane was on her way home from a difficult day at work when it started to rain and she was caught without an umbrella. She wanted to cry, but it was against her nature to display emotions in public. So she ran across the street and pushed her way through the varnished oak entrance into a bookstore. She stopped inside the door and closed her eyes. Her head lilted to one side as she gasped quietly for breath.

"Just let it rain." His voice was smooth, but Jane quickly stood erect. Her eyes snapped open, and she was in control of herself in less than a moment. "Sometimes you just can't stop the rain." His head was leaning slightly to one side as he looked inquisitively into her eyes. "I came in here to get out of the rain, too." He explained with a slightly boyish grin. "We can't stop it, but we don't have to get wet, either."

"No," Jane agreed cautiously.

"Something's got you down besides the weather. You don't have to talk to me about it. We could just sit inside here, drink coffee, and watch it pour. I'll buy the coffee."

"You don't have to be nice. I appreciate your concern, but I'll be fine."

"Wouldn't you do the same for me if the roles were reversed?"

"No," Jane replied flatly, but there was something disarming about him.

"Then this is destiny." There was that smile again, but broader. "It had to happen this way. You and I both came in here for a reason."

"To get out of the rain," Jane replied as she finally returned his smile.

"Right," he agreed. "So let's get out of the rain together."

The coffee was hot, the conversation was warm, and they let it rain while they watched the cascading water deluge the outside the building. Sitting comfortably inside they drank coffee and talked for hours. When it stopped raining, they went for dinner. That was the beginning.

For two years Jane dated Sammy. The relationship was comfortable, and Jane didn't think about other things when she was with him. He was like an old pair of jeans that she could slip into when she wanted to relax. Often she would pause just outside his house and lean against the door, knowing that she was about to see him. When she was anxious, she would put the entire weight of her body on the door until he opened it.

It was a heavy door, made of a dark hardwood. The faded blue paint was chipped and flaked off with each touch. There was something about the vulnerability of the finish that made Jane desire touching it more. Each time she passed the door, she caressed the grooves with her fingertips or the back of her hand. Molly always knew when Jane had gone to visit Sammy: the splattering of blue paint chips on Jane's fingers and clothing gave her away. Jane would also sing quietly to herself when she came home. Usually this was some Cole Porter tune that Sammy was listening to when Jane was there. Sammy had definite opinions on music, and he wasn't likely to listen to anything that had been written in recent years. "The atrophy of sound" is how Sammy referred to contemporary music.

After two years Jane began to understand that Sammy was almost like a hiding place for her. She started to see the relationship as something outside the real world and, being ever sensible, Jane decided that she needed to stop seeing Sammy and find someone else. They had gotten along well. There were no arguments. But Jane knew that if she wanted to advance her career she would need someone who could help her. Sammy didn't like business social events. He didn't like dressing formally, and he didn't like the air of pretense.

When she and Sammy said goodbye, Jane stood outside the door of his house and allowed the tears to stream silently down her face. She could hear him throwing books against the wall one by one -- books that came from the store where they met. Although the sound was faint, Jane could hear that he was crying also.

There are certain doors in life that, once closed, can never be reopened. This was one of them. Jane paused to listen to the sounds echoing from the other side of Sammy's door. She stood there long enough to hear the noises fade and then finally disappear. Then she walked away, knowing that she must.

When Jane told Molly that she had broken off her relationship with Sammy, Molly called Jane an idiot, as well as several other names that Molly usually reserved for her least favorite politicians. Jane looked at the books on her shelf and felt like throwing them, but she refrained and stood erectly.

"It's over," she announced with firmness. Molly got up and left the room, slamming the door to the study behind her. Two panes of glass shattered in one of the doors. Molly turned around abruptly.

"There's one for you and one for him." Molly was crying as if it were her own heart breaking. She felt everything deeply. She had cared for Sammy because Jane cared for him. Molly grieved the way that Jane wished she could grieve for herself, and Jane loved Molly for it. Jane comforted Molly with long embraces, and Molly continued to weep for days. Jane never did fix the broken glass. The missing panes reminded her too much of Molly's affection.

It was in Jane's study, in the privacy of the room with the paned glass doors, that Molly usually discussed new career opportunities. Molly changed jobs and careers often. She would discuss her latest idea with her more stable and sober-minded sister and weigh the advice accordingly. Then there was the time when Molly was scheduled to interview for a position and she decided not to go inside once she saw the front door of the office.

"It was painted to look like marble. There's something

about a faux finish that I just don't trust. It's misleading," Molly protested.

"That's like judging a book by its cover. The door has nothing to do with what's inside."

"It has everything to do with it!" Molly stood up from the over stuffed chair in which she was haphazardly reclined. She kicked the side of it with the toe of her shoe, slightly tearing the taupe fabric. "He was giving the impression that the door was made of marble. But it wasn't! And who'd make a door out of marble, anyway? It'd be too heavy to push open. That's nonsensical! I can't work for someone who's full of nonsense!"

"You're right. Someone should have sense, and it obviously isn't going to be you." Jane couldn't help rolling her eyes. As someone with artistic inclinations, Molly had no room to complain about something like this.

It was a restful Saturday, and the sisters played cards to pass the time in the afternoon. They sat in Jane's study, with the pale yellow afternoon light illuminating the sage green paint on the walls.

"Are you seeing anyone?" Molly asked with an affected air of indifference from behind her hand of cards.

She moved several cards around, as if reorganizing her hand. But the cards were still in no particular order.

They both knew that Jane almost never went out. Her social life had taken a serious downturn as she spent more and more time at work. Jane knew where the conversation was headed, and so she toyed with Molly.

"My romantic entanglements are in the wind. The wind has a volatile, artistic personality. He's faithful in that he always returns, no matter how long he's absent."

"If the wind is a man, he's probably blowing up every skirt in town!" Molly laughed at her own joke. Jane pretended to be serious.

"There's something erotic in the way that he's always present, yet constantly blowing in and out of my life. I feel happy when he's here. When he's not, I look forward to when he comes back."

"Like Sammy?"

"Don't go there." Jane's tone was suddenly firm.

"Maybe you should call him, Jane."

"Even if I was wrong for leaving him, I can't go back there. It could never be the same again." Jane threw her weight back in her chair and let the cards fall from her hands. "I admit that I miss him sometimes. But I had to make a choice, and I made it."

"Sometimes people are wrong. Sometimes I'm wrong. I'm sorry if I'm making you angry. But you were different with him."

"I wasn't me."

"You were. But when you were with him, you let yourself feel things that you usually try to ignore. Don't snuff out the life inside of yourself. Live it. This is the only life you have, and you're going through it without poetry and without … life, really. You're wasting most of it sitting around here. If I ever get cancer or get sick or if anything ever happens to me, I want you to remember this and promise me that you'll do it. If there comes ever a time when I can't live, I want you to do it for me."

"Nothing will happen to you. You're so dramatic! And besides, I could never live like you," Jane laughed at the thought. "You're larger than life."

"I'm not asking you to live like me. I'm just asking you to live. You're so practical about everything. Don't you ever wish that you could build a doorway that leads to the moon? That's what Sammy was for you. He took you outside yourself so that you could really be yourself. You were never more alive than when you were with him."

Without answering, Jane got up from her seat and walked outside. It was early evening, and the sun was still shining. She sat down on the concrete steps and looked around.

The foliage was just beginning to yellow. Like eager revolutionaries, a few of the changing leaves had severed themselves from their branches and already plunged earthward.

Jane and Molly had always liked to sit on the front steps and watch the faded branches at this time of the year. The afternoon sun enhanced the gold and diminished the green appearance of the trees further. Jane loved this. It was a sign of change.

Molly bounced down the front steps of the porch and threw her oversized purse into the back seat of her old red convertible.

"Stop moping!" She shouted as she climbed into the car. The car door creaked loudly as she opened it and groaned with every motion, like a woman in childbirth. Molly jerked the faded red door closed with both hands, throwing all her weight into the action. The noise of scraping metal increased in pitch and volume until it ended in a sudden crunch.

"I'll call you later," Molly shouted with a smile as she pushed a few loose strands of hair from her face. She quickly threw the car into gear and sped off.

Jane breathed deeply as she studied the tree limbs hanging over the street tenderly stroking each vehicle passing underneath, much as a lover's fingers would affectionately tousle the beloved's hair. Just as the slightly cool wind tousled her own hair.

There was a rush of sound precipitating every stirring breeze. The wind caressed Jane's skin through the woven fibers her sweater, as it moved the fallen leaves into further disarray. The weather was flirting with her, she thought. Maybe her romance wasn't with the wind, but instead with autumn. While some people associate that time of year with death, Molly and Jane saw it as a preparation for the new life of spring. Because of this, there was no pain or sadness in the autumn for these sisters. To them this time of year was both poignant and beautiful.

Jane was studying the colors of a leaf when she heard

the sudden noise of screeching tires quickly followed by a thunderous crash of metal and shattering glass. She looked up but couldn't see any cars. She rose to her feet in order to look farther down the avenue. As she walked down the steps of the house, she heard the bang of the front door slamming abruptly behind her. She quickly turned around to study the pale green doorway leading inside her home. No one was there. Perhaps it was the wind. But then, Molly always did like to exit with a bang.

When Jane walked back through the doorway to her house, she knew without looking that it was a different door for her. No one had to tell her that Molly had died in that car accident. She already knew. As Jane stepped inside the house she felt the stillness, the quiet, the emptiness, and all the pain. Then she knew that Sammy had been right: sometimes you just can't stop the rain. For Jane, this was one of those times.

I watch the moon's luminous breath dissipate into the night sky as he finishes the story. He glances down at his sil very goatee. Then, as if dissatisfied with his appearance, he shoots rods of golden light through his beard, combing the ethereal tresses with his own light. I'm enchanted by his very presence, and though I know that he wants me to speak, I cannot vocalize. I wait in silence for him to speak again. When he does, I feel his voice and his light resonate through me. He is a powerful and beautiful presence.

"There are some doors in life which you cannot, yourself, open or close," he explains. "These only open long enough to give one a glimpse into the eternal, and then these doors slam closed before you can see anything clearly enough to know your destiny for certain. This is what Molly meant when she talked about a doorway to the moon: finding a path to the unreachable."

"Yet there are times when the unreachable will reach out to us." I smile shyly upwards at him. I know that he has opened such a door for me this evening. He, himself, is my very own doorway to the moon.

Chapter
Three

Painting the New Moon

"I sometimes think that I should like to be an artist and paint lovely things," I mention one evening when the moon is particularly brilliant. "I might even paint you," I add flirtatiously.

" 'The artist who is not also a craftsman is no good; but alas, most of our artists are nothing else.'" He pauses; as if he's still listening to himself speak. Perhaps he can hear his own voice resonating through space. "Goethe brings to mind the question of ability."

"What about ability?"

"Do you have any?   Or do you simply intend to paint your feelings." He emphasizes the last word with disdain.

 "What's wrong with feelings? A great many people have feelings for you. Though perhaps they might not -- if they knew how you mock them."

" 'One must not always think that feeling is everything. Art is nothing without form.' Flaubert." The moon loves to quote. He watches the intimate details of everyone's life. He feels as if he knows us all, and when he quotes famous people, it's his manner of subtly reminding me of this. He blows a stream of celestial air to make form and pattern within his shimmering breath. I watch the swirling circles rotate and then twinkle softly into nothingness. "And," he adds with that wry grin he likes to display when he's in his waxing crescent phase, "Form is paramount. It is secondary only to composition in art."

"You've known a great many artists."

"I've known all the great artists, and they have known me. But greatness and success are not equivalent. Some of the most accomplished artists could not earn enough to sustain themselves. Van Gogh who, by the way, was a lovely man to chat with on a breezy summer night only sold one painting in his entire life. But he was brilliant." The moon dims slightly, and he suddenly looks sad. I watch him sink a little in the sky as he whispers, "I do miss him."

"He's well-recognized now."

"Yes. If only he could have seen what his work was to become. But fame and fortune are both capricious mistresses. They mirror the fickleness so often found within the human heart." He closes his eyes for a moment. When he opens them again, the flood of moonbeams pours out brilliantly in every direction. I can feel the surge of his light flowing over me and caressing my bare skin. The sensation fades quickly, and he begins to speak again.

"I am reminded of a story of two artists." He pauses long enough for me to demonstrate my interest. I walk farther out onto the terrace and turn one of the verdant wrought iron chairs toward his face. Once seated, I begin sipping my tea and gaze upward into his light as he begins the story.

These artists were great friends. They lived in Paris, like so many of my artist friends. The first was known by the name of Emile. He was a passionate man whose mood changed faster than any wind. He was in and out of love often. When he was in love, it was deep and his passion consumed him. The world had more flavor then. The colors had more depth for him. When he was out of love, he was distant with the world.

The second artist was named Henri. He was a native of Paris, born in one of the quiet streets of the Latin Quarter. He loved to paint the countryside. There was nothing more beautiful to him than nature. He painted the countryside exactly as he saw it, invoking the axiom that God's work needs no improvement.

Emile and Henri met often at the neighborhood café. I should say that they went there often when they had the money for coffee. Like all artists, this pair went through times of hardship. When one of the two was doing well, he would often buy coffee or a meal for the other. The two supported each other both financially and artistically, although their painting styles were quite different. They discussed their differences and tried to learn from each other, but occasionally they would argue fiercely over some technique. Once, in a fit of rage, Emile smashed a bottle of wine over the back of a bistro chair during lunch.

"The wine," Henri moaned. "Don't take it out on the wine. It's good wine."

"A nice alizarin shade," Emile agreed with sudden remorse. Henri watched the shape of the liquid streaming across the gray sidewalk. The wine had scattered in all directions, and the pieces of the bottle dispersed evenly on the ground, like the face of a sundial.

"You could get that shade by mixing some cadmium red with a violet hue," Henri commented.

"Which cadmium? You'd do better to use the crimson and deepen the hue. It would look better to the eye."

"But the wine has more red than purple."

"Yes. But the purple will add depth to the composition. The visual effect will be stronger."

"Ach!" Henri exclaimed as he swatted his hand in front of his face with an air of disgust. Emile sighed deeply, expressively. Then he sat down abruptly, as if some divine puppeteer had dropped all his strings.

"Yes, the wine is more red in appearance. But violet will sell the picture." Emile suddenly sat upwards. "Unless … " He leaned forward on the table and put his face close to Henri's. "Unless I use a deeper cadmium shade and give the wine the appearance of spilt blood."

Emile fell backwards in his chair contemplatively. He studied the pattern of the wine on the sidewalk. He slowly lifted his foot and placed the tip of his heel into the puddle of liquid. Then he drew his heal out of the pool and started a trickle of wine flowing in a new direction. "The symbolism ... " He stared at the wine, as if he could see some magical reflection speaking to him from within the mass of fluid. He suddenly jumped up again and announced that he was going to paint the scene.

"Paint it, you fool. No one will buy it," Henri replied calmly with an air of wisdom. But someone did buy it. In fact, Emile was financially more successful than Henri, though most critics readily agree that Henri was the greater master of the two. Henri knew this, also, and it bothered him. He watched Emile's success as it flourished, and he felt painfully jealous of it. Henri went to Mass each Sunday and prayed that he could be just half as successful as Emile just enough to make a decent living. But no matter how many candles he lit, Henri's paintings didn't sell. He resorted to painting portraits so that he could earn enough to eat.

Henri's portraits had a very lifelike quality about them. He was very precise in depicting his subjects. He used just the right shades, tones, and glazes to depict his subject exactly. Yet, many of his patrons refused to pay for the work once it was completed. After about two years of painting the most exquisite likenesses, Henri was still as poor as ever. His studio was lined with works of art for which his patrons had refused payment. Emile came to Henri's studio and marveled at the craftsmanship.

"You flatter me," Henri replied flatly.

"You're discouraged. We've all been that way. But these paintings are marvelous. The subjects look as if they could begin conversing with us right now."

"Perhaps they could explain why they were rejected." Henri sighed deeply as he folded his arms. "If only they could talk."

"All paintings talk," Emile retorted in a matter-of-fact tone as he continued to admire the pattern of brushstrokes on the canvas. "They can't help talking. They're the voice of the artist's soul." He touched his fingers to his smooth chin thoughtfully and then glanced at his friend. "I'm going to the country to paint some landscapes. Come with me." Henri shrugged listlessly to show his indifference to the suggestion. "Come," Emile continued, "You love the country. We can paint the farmers in their wheat fields by day and the stars at night. It will be wonderful!"

"I don't have the money for passage …"

"You're my guest. I will bring supplies for both of us. It's settled then. We leave in the morning." Emile paused long enough to briefly kiss Henri's cheek before he left. Henri devoured his remaining loaf of bread and slowly finished off the last of his cheese. Then he began packing his things for the journey. He had no reason to stay in Paris and he didn't want to be home when the landlady came for the rent in two days.

Emile was lively and excited from the moment of their arrival in the countryside. There were a number of beautiful women in the small town, and he was in love with all of them. He painted vivid scenes with brighter yellows, deeper blues, and violet shadows instead of simple gray tones. His paintings were imaginative and encompassed elements not present in the pastoral scenes. Instead of painting the simple grass field he saw, he added a beautiful dark-haired woman in repose beneath the sage green shade of an olive tree. His paintings were filled with color and symbolism.

True to his maxim, Henri painted the world as he saw it. His paintings were slowly executed with deft brushstrokes. He used subtle shading to make the painting look more as if it were a window looking out upon the scene before him. Henri's technique made the painting look three-dimensional and alive.

"It looks so realistic that I feel as if I could walk right into that painting," Emile commented on his fellow artist's work. Emile admired Henri's work greatly.

"But who would want to?" Henri was still quite depressed over his financial situation. He could not afford to buy his own paints or brushes anymore. Emile provided everything that Henri used to paint with on this excursion. Henri felt a sense of indebtedness mixed with jealousy that Emile earned enough from his work to provide for both of them.

"Come. We'll have a magnificent dinner. Then we will come back tonight and paint the stars." Emile was optimistic. With so many beautiful women nearby, he was filled with love for the whole world. He was so ecstatic that he sometimes broke into song while he was painting. If Emile's singing wasn't bad enough (and it was), the sheer outpouring of joy irritated Henri into silencing him with a cutting remark.

During dinner Emile praised everything: the wine, the food, the service. He had great things to say about the world. It was all so wonderful to him. He was passionately in love with no one in particular.

"Don't be so happy, or I shall take to my bed," Henri threatened with a faint sneer.

"Why not be joyful? We can live. We can love. We can paint. We have it all!"

"You have it all. I can paint. But I cannot sell my paintings. I might as well not paint at all." Henri stared at his food. He wanted to eat, but he could not bring himself to take more than a few bites. The meal was delicious, but Henri felt as if each mouthful burned his throat as he swallowed.

"You could sell your paintings." Emile nodded reticently as he spoke.

"How?" Henri waved his fork through the air in small, circular motions. "Why is it that I can't even sell what I'm commissioned to paint?"

"You paint beautifully. I've never seen better technique in any artist. If I only had more of your talent, Henri …"

"You wouldn't make so much money!" Henri interjected as he raised his fork with an air of triumph. Emile nodded in agreement, then lowered his dark eyes and spoke softly to his dear friend.

"You paint what you see. People won't pay for that, Henri. They have eyes. They can look for themselves. They don't want what they already have in front of them. You must give them something else."

"I paint truth." Henri shrugged dispassionately. His solemn face became warmer in expression. "Isn't that what it's all about?"

"Art is about beauty. People can see truth. We must show them beauty."

"Truth, itself, is beautiful."

"Truth can be ugly. It can be painful," Emile persisted.

"And there can be beauty in pain if it's real!"

"You are fooled. No one thinks that pain is beautiful." Emile's temper was beginning to flare. He felt the effect of the wine blazing in his skin. Suddenly the night seemed warmer than it did a moment ago, and even the small candle on the table added to the heat. Henri felt the fever of the moment also. His usually calm disposition flared in response to Emile's passion.

"The cross! What about Calvary? Who doesn't weep at the beauty of Christ giving his life on the cross?" Henri quickly slammed his fist down as he finished speaking. The fork, which he had already forgotten, ejected from his hand, landing on a nearby table. Neither artist noticed the loss of the utensil. They stared each other down with a vengeance. The moment of tension extended to almost a full minute as Emile's dark eyes pierced into Henri's soft blue-green irises. Then Emile's expression abruptly softened, and he spoke in a practical tone.

"Priests can afford to weep. The rest of us need to earn a living," he remarked.

"Ach!' Then Henri smiled wearily as he continued to speak, "If only we didn't need to eat."

"If you want to make money, you must paint what the patron finds beautiful. Real beauty exists when truth is aptly defined. Not realistically defined, but appropriately defined. Take for example your portrait of the woman with the crooked nose."

"Mademoiselle Rastignac." Henri smiled with a half-knowing, half-mirthful air.

"A crooked nose must be straightened. Yes, in reality the nose is crooked. But in truth, the woman wishes it to be straight. So we paint it straight or at least straighter than it is and the woman is content. This is art: part reality, part imagination, true to the desires of the subject -- or patron. The result is what others find beautiful." Emile grinned as he waved his hand in front of his face. Henri sighed over the creative difference, but he couldn't argue with success. "Come," Emile continued with his attitude of love for the world around him. "We'll go paint the moon!"

"It's the new moon, you fool," Henri smiled affectionately as he spoke.

"Painting what people want is like painting the new moon."

"There's no moon tonight." Henri was now laughing exuberantly.

"Exactly." Emile smiled happily as he waited for Henri's fit of mirth to quell, then he continued. "It isn't to be seen, so we paint it as we wish to see it at that moment."

"Ah."

"You still don't understand."

"No."

"When the moon is in this phase, it isn't visible to the human eye. The night is black, and the moon is completely dark. There is nothing to be seen. So we must tell the viewers what they want to see."

"And what do they wish to see?"

"Something beautiful that they can't see at the moment." Emile winked at a voluptuous waitress as she passed the table. She paused briefly as she strolled by the table, her skirt rustling loudly as she moved.

"A full moon?" Henri asked hesitantly.

"Perhaps." Emile smiled again at the waitress. "But maybe a crescent shape would provide the appropriate rhythm and harmony for the scenery. We must assess each situation and determine exactly what makes it beautiful."

"Let's go." Henri rose from his chair hastily, his face full of determination and a hint of optimism. "Let's not paint tonight, but let's go and find things to paint."

And so they strolled down the banks of the river,

through the small town, past the neatly plowed fields, through overgrown pastures, and just about everywhere obtainable by foot. They walked for most of the night, pausing to discuss what sort of moon should be painted in each scene and where in the sky it should be placed.

But when it came time to paint, Henri's composition looked more like a photograph and Emile's looked more like a dream. Given the choice, people will buy dreams more often than reality. While Henri could meticulously duplicate anything in the created world, he could not deliver to people what they wanted most: their aspirations.

Years later when Henri died, it was in poverty. In a fit of depression shortly before his death, he destroyed his studio and a great number of his paintings. Today there are very few of this master's works that escaped those flames inspired by despair. The blaze that consumed his lifetime of painting warmed his hands and chilled his soul. Once the paintings had been reduced to ashes in his fireplace, Henri felt an even greater sense of hopelessness. He had neither success nor his art during his last hours. He died quietly in his sleep.

Emile mourned the loss of his friend, as well as the

loss of Henri's masterpieces. And while Emile's success continued to thrive, he never ceased wishing that he possessed more of Henri's talent.

As he finished the story, his smile was half contentment and half remorse. The moon has great affection for artists. Perhaps he knows how much these souls admire him. I certainly can't explain all the moon's habits or choices. Even after our long friendship, he's still as much a mystery to me as we are to him. I don't wish to disturb his thoughts, and so I sit quietly enjoying his gentle light.

I watch as the moon exchanges greetings with a far-off comet. The language is unearthly and foreign to me, but it is beautiful. The sounds are more like music than words to my ears. As I walk back inside my house, he says good night to me. His voice is still musical and resonates through my whole body. I will sleep well, just as he wishes.

Chapter
Four

Gibbous Dreams

The moon does not sit still, even when he appears to be still from our earthly perspective. He is both in motion and the source of motion for others. He moves the lunatic to dance the chaotic tarantella. He also moves the tides to a more uniform rhythm. Neither the lunatic nor the tide can resist his pull. He is magical.

But the moon is mischievous when he imparts dreams to both the fortunate and unfortunate. His moonbeams may strike the heart of the innocent while they sleep and take seed there during the night.

"It must have been you," I remark softly as I awake to the soft caress of his light and recall my dream. He nods vaguely. His motion is almost imperceptible tonight. He moves faintly and speaks softly.

"I wanted to talk with you." His voice is steady, but

quiet. I sit up slowly and attempt to shake the remains of my dreams from my consciousness. His gentle light is cool on my skin and warm in my soul. It's a balm of peace to my abruptly stirred mind. I gradually make my way out of bed and toward the window. The curtains are sheer, but I pull them aside to see my friend more clearly. Then I open the window and sit down as the cold air rushes into the room. My thoughts are still slow, but the slight chill increases their rapidity.

"What about?" I breathe deeply. Each inhalation enhances my alertness and curiosity.

"I spoke to you in your dream." He smiles with that familiar mixture of tenderness and condescension.

"I wish you wouldn't do that. I can hardly tell if the voice I hear is yours or mine."

"I know." He is pleased. His face becomes a little triumphant, and his aura expands brilliantly for a few moments. His expression returns to one of tenderness, and his eyes reflect the fullness of his gibbous phase.

"Were you lonely?"

"How could I be?" He is taken aback and slightly defensive. "I can talk to anyone. There are other humans, you know. And there are millions of stars, each of which would revel in a good conversation with me. After all, they're very curious about the earth and I observe it so closely." The moon is sometimes a capricious friend. He knows how we mortals desire to know him, and yet he doesn't always like to admit his attachment to any one of us. This is simply another of his moods.

"Yet you chose to talk to me."

"I can still choose to talk to anyone I please." He's somewhat indignant, and his light dims as he turns his countenance from me. I wait silently for a few moments, wondering if this mood will pass. I glance at the time. It's after midnight. Finally I speak again.

"And yet it is I that you've woken up from a very deep slumber." He slowly moves his light in my direction, as if with apprehension. I watch the rays of light gradually reach toward me and extend themselves into my room once again. Their touch is overwhelmingly pleasant, and I smile. "Why do you speak in dreams?" I ask when he has returned my smile and I know that the capricious mood has passed like the drifting clouds that sometimes obscure his face.

"Because I can." He smiles more broadly and begins a story.

Dreams are so little understood by mankind. Still, there are books and theories and entire works of art based on dreams. Dreams are sometimes considered good, sometimes evil. Some dreams are feared, and others are considered to be as innocuous as the air you breathe. But air is necessary to life. And life without dreams would be suffocating. The only thing that humans understand less than their dreams are their own hearts. The two are intertwined.

There are those who know what they want in this life, but they don't know how to get it. Then again, what a person wants and what the person needs are seldom synchronous concepts. Dreams reveal any discrepancy. The nocturnal workings of the slumbering mind are honest. There is no place to hide inside of one's own heart; this is the place in which dreams dwell. A person's dreams will reveal the true condition of the soul.

There are dreams of both the waking and sleeping variety. The dreams you have when you sleep are infinitely more reliable. These are the dreams that cannot be tainted by consciousness. Most people have both types of dreams, and this was the case with Ricardo.

Ricardo was a young man who dreamed of being a professional baseball player. He had this dream often. It started when he was still quite small. He fantasized during the daytime when he should have been doing algebra or other practical things. At night the visions continued much the same. In his dream, Ricardo was bathed in the floodlights of an enormous stadium, and the sound of cheering resounded in his ears. He had just finished rounding the bases and he could feel warm streams of perspiration rolling down the small of his back. The breezy night air would push the cap from his head and then reach through his dark hair to gently stroke his scalp. When Ricardo leaned over to retrieve his cap from the infield, he would hear a small boy shouting from a seat behind the dugout. Ricardo would walk over to the brown-haired boy, holding the soiled cap in his hand. When the boy smiled, Ricardo would give him the cap, brushing off a small amount of dirt and grass from the brim, as he did so. As soon as Ricardo released his grip on the cap he would awake, feeling startled.

Whenever he thought of the dream, Ricardo replayed the crowd noises and cheering fans in his mind. He knew that baseball was a team sport, but he was certain that he would be a star. This, he thought, was his destiny. So he worked hard to make it come true. He bought a small trampoline and put it up against the fence in his back yard. He used this help develop a strong, precise throwing arm by pitching the ball at the target painted in the center. He asked his dad to play catch with him whenever his dad was available, but that wasn't often. He practiced batting both right - and left-handed so that he had a strong swing and good timing from either side of the plate. He would practice hitting balls with his friends, but his friends quickly lost interest in retrieving the balls that Ricardo hit so far away. Still, he looked for any opportunity to play. When he wasn't playing, he was usually watching a game on television, analyzing and rehearsing the motions of each player. He studied the coordination of movements between players. It was like a symphony to him. Just as it is with music, the tides, or the seasons, rhythm and timing determine everything in baseball. Without these two things, the game is chaos. So Ricardo worked on developing the rhythm of the game so that it would become a part of his own internal clock.

He started playing on youth league teams at an early age. He put up with poor coaches, crazed parents, and inept players. When one mother stormed the field and pulled her twins from a game, Ricardo stood in the outfield and laughed good-naturedly. The mother was furious that one of her sons had been placed in right field. So she grabbed both her right fielder and shortstop by the backs of their shirts and marched them off the field while shouting obscenities at the coach. Then she drove her children home, leaving her bewildered husband on the bleachers to watch the rest of the team forfeit the game because they didn't have enough players to finish it. When Ricardo's crescendo of laughter finally diminished, he quickly began throwing the ball to other players. If there would be no game, they would still practice for the next one. There would be nothing to get in his way of developing his skills.

Youth league is a sport unto itself, and each coach has

his pick of players. A coach will often use the same players during a game, and this isn't always based on ability. You were more likely to be assigned the position of your choice if your father was a friend of the coach. So Ricardo didn't necessarily play every game, but he went to each practice and put up with every beer-gutted coach he came across. He knew that the only way to learn baseball is to play it. One cannot acquire rhythm and timing through observation. Every muscle in the player's body must learn exactly when to flex in relation to the other muscles in order to gain those precious fractions of seconds needed to make an out or score a run. The player's body is more than a physical machine; it's a timepiece that strives to coordinate its own movements with precision.

Ricardo's dedication and endless practice sessions paid off. During his freshman year in high school, Ricardo made the varsity team and played all four years of high school. He spent more time practicing than any of the other players, and while he hated calisthenics, he did them with enthusiasm. After every game the other team members would drive up and down a place known as "the strip." The entire quarter-mile of the strip consisted of seven buildings: the Sweetwater Saloon, the grocery store, the First (and only) Baptist Church, Farber Insurance Company, the courthouse, a dental clinic, and the post office. The basic purpose of driving down this strip was to see who else was driving down it and sometimes to meet girls. Ricardo never went out on these excursions after the games. He took a lot of teasing because of it, but he didn't care. He would rather get to bed early or watch a game on television. He thought that driving down the strip was something that people did when they had the rest of their lives to waste. Ricardo had a talent to develop.

When Ricardo graduated from high school, he went to a prestigious university on a baseball scholarship. He not only played well for the school, he broke most of the existing batting records. He could hit just about any pitch and hit it hard. There is no question that Ricardo had exceptional skills: Twenty-five years later, the records he set are still unbroken.

While he was in college, Ricardo started dating. Many were attracted to his lean muscular figure, but he settled on one who was captivated by his ambition. Her name was Maura. She admired and supported him, and yet it was

Ricardo's ambition that later drove them apart.

"You care more for that worn-out glove than you care for me!" She exclaimed before she left.

"I knew that you'd never understand."

"No, Ricardo. You're the one who doesn't understand. You're driven to give yourself to something that can never love you back. One day you'll wake up feeling empty and wondering why. Then you'll think about what I said and know that I was right."

Ricardo moved on, as he always did. With his usual resolution, he picked himself up and concentrated on his game. He occasionally dated other women, but he missed Maura. He felt content when he was with her. She had been fun and supportive up until their last, not to mention only, argument. Ricardo had broken out of his strict routine and gone places that he had never been before. He even ventured into museums and attended a few concerts. Ricardo learned about the world outside baseball. More important than the entertainment that he discovered when he was with her, Maura taught him about life. She was the only true companion he had ever known. He had talked to her openly. He missed her friendship as much as her love, but he didn't know why. In the end he felt that she had betrayed him by challenging his dream.

Ricardo was lonely, but he filled his life with baseball, as he had done before. Those who watched him play would never have known that someone who could hit with such power could also feel so depleted at times. When Ricardo played, it was with all the enthusiasm that the rest of his life lacked.

After college, he spent a little time on a minor league team, but within a year he was playing in the majors. Each time he stepped onto the field, he felt as if he was returning home. He would drink up the stadium atmosphere. The air smells different on a baseball field. There was always the faint scent of cut grass and hot dogs during a game. But there was something else. The subtle fragrance of dirt from the infield, the smells of rosin, chewing tobacco, sweat, and leather gloves all intermingled into a strange perfume. Ricardo loved this. Each time a cloud of dust rose up from a dramatic play in the infield and the scent wafted near him, he felt new energy flowing through his body. He truly lived for the game.

Ricardo's team did very well that year. Each time they

won a game, he felt as if his dream was coming a little closer to reality. He still had that same dream, but he didn't wake up as startled as he did when he was younger. As his life moved forward into that great fog we call the future, the clouds didn't seem nearly as thick as when he dreamed of them from far away. In fact, things appeared far less obscure to him. That's the funny thing about the future. When we finally reach it, it doesn't look exactly like what we expected because the distance of the past distorts the images.

It was during the final playoff game that Ricardo finally lived his fantasy. During the bottom of the tenth inning, Ricardo was at bat with a man on second base and two outs. Everyone in the stadium knew that the moment was critical. This game would determine whether or not Ricardo would be playing the World Series. Ricardo felt nervous, but he closed his eyes and inhaled the energizing scent of the game. This was his life force. He could breathe easily.

He paused to knock some imaginary dirt from his left shoe with the tip of the bat. Then he checked the sole of his right shoe. It was clean, but he tapped the inside of that shoe with the bat, also. Ricardo took another deep breath before pulling the bat over his left shoulder and crouching into his stance.

Ricardo focused on the pitcher's left hand. He studied the rapid movements of the pitcher turning the ball within his glove. Any good pitcher will go through the same ritual of motion before each pitch. It keeps the batter from determining the type of pitch before he sees the ball coming toward him. The movement of the ball is something like falling dominoes: once the chain of motion has begun, it will continue until something disrupts the flow. When a batter makes good contact, the motion simply changes direction but it keeps going. A good pitcher prevents this from happening.

Ricardo saw the pitcher come to the set position, but his eyes focused on the throwing arm. He watched the arm rapidly come from behind the pitcher's body and release the ball. Ricardo didn't move. He couldn't even will his muscles to flex and swing. There was no time to mentally consider the pitch and make a judgment. His body simply knew that it didn't like the appearance of that rotating orb as it approached. As the sphere crossed the plate, Ricardo watched it drop, and the umpire declared ball one.

Ricardo stood up from his batting stance and put all his weight on one foot. He checked the sole of the opposite shoe, as if it might have collected some extraneous dirt from the speed of the pitch that had just whirled through the air before him. He struck the bat gently against the instep of each shoe once again for good measure and then resumed his batting stance. All of his awareness was focused on the pitcher. Nothing existed for him at that moment but the solitary figure on the mound. He studied the left arm as it came up and over to release the ball. He watched the beautiful symmetry of the lines depicting a nice backspin, but he didn't swing and he couldn't explain why. Something inside him felt that the pitch was too high, and when his arm muscles began to flex, he could not bring himself to complete the swing. He watched the pitch cross the plate a little high but within the strike zone. Hearing the sound of the umpire call it a strike only added to Ricardo's frustration of wishing he had followed through on the swing. But the pitch was high, and he couldn't afford to hit anything that would make an easy catch. The strike was out of his mind as quickly as it had crossed the plate. He didn't dwell on it.

Ricardo stepped back from the plate again and grabbed the brim of his cap. He released the brim, but then grabbed it again and removed the cap. He knew that his body had been trained into the rhythm of the game and would choose the correct action. He smoothed his dark brown hair away from his face before replacing the cap and stepping back up to the plate. Once again, he concentrated on the pitcher's throwing arm. The pitcher went through the same preparatory motions, but all Ricardo saw was that left arm as it came around just slightly to the side.

The curve went down and away. Ricardo had connected with the motion of the ball from the first moment that he saw the pitcher's wrist break. His body moved in rhythm with the flow of that sphere and his timing was impeccable. His reflexes started moving before his brain even considered what kind of pitch was coming toward him. It wasn't until he was in full swing and making contact that he could see what his body already knew: the ball was rotating on an axis that mimicked earth's own rotation. Ricardo's bat met the ball over the plate and reversed the momentum all the way out of the park. The game was over.

Of course, he was elated. As he finished rounding the bases the entire team met him at the plate. The two runs he brought in won the game and they were going to the World Series. The team hugged and patted Ricardo, and perhaps with all the excitement, Ricardo thought that he imagined it, but the first-base coach did kiss him on the cheek. Most of the team headed for the locker room to celebrate, but Ricardo stood on the infield near the third-base line. He stared up into the floodlights. He expected one last rush of satisfaction, but in the glare of those bright lights he felt a chill that didn't come from the night air. He looked at the seats above the dugout, as if he expected to see the little boy, but there was no one matching the description of the boy in his dream. Ricardo felt the emptiness more acutely than ever. The applause resounded in his ears. He listened to the thunderous noise and heard a few isolated cheers mentioning his name. But he looked into the crowd and saw no one. There were thousands of faceless people, all of whom knew his name. But he didn't know any of them, and there was no real comfort in the sound of applause. The noise only made him feel lonelier, and he wondered where the joy of the game had gone.

Ricardo went to sleep that night, but he didn't rest well. He got up several times, and he stayed awake for hours thinking about his performance. Was every move executed to the best of his ability? Was there a problem with his timing or the equipment? Why didn't he feel the sense of triumph that he thought he would feel? When he finally slept that night, he had another dream, but not one of games, floodlights, or applause. There was no spectacular play in front of thousands of people. This time he dreamt that he walked out of a vacant stadium and the emptiness stayed behind him to echo in the grandstands. The next thing he knew he was on a quiet field, and everything appeared smaller, even the players.

The dream disturbed Ricardo, as truth often does. He thought about it continually. For a while, he blamed this dream for what happened next: during the first game of the World Series he injured his shoulder. He made a difficult catch and then fell as he tried to throw the ball infield too quickly. He tore a group of muscles in his shoulder. The crowd roared, but he immediately knew that there was a serious problem. The pain was unlike any he had ever felt. Ricardo's career was suddenly over. His team won the World Series, but it was a bittersweet triumph for Ricardo. He didn't play for most of the series. Since this injury occurred before sports medicine had advanced enough to develop a corrective surgery for the problem, there wasn't much that any doctor could do. At the end of the series, Ricardo was no longer a member of a major league ballclub. He retired at the age of twenty-four.

Ricardo went back to his hometown to sulk. For weeks he mourned the loss of his career. He had worked his whole life for something. Now he felt as if fate had snatched a promised reward from his grasp. There were times when he recalled Maura's words, and he hated her for saying those things, because they appeared more than true. The game could not love him back, and the fans would quickly transfer their devotion to the next rising star.

For a long time he did nothing but scold himself for allowing his anxiety to upset his timing: he had made the throw when he wasn't balanced. He had rushed the action, and the motion wasn't coordinated. There was no way that he could have gotten adequate momentum behind the ball without good rhythm and timing. He replayed the scene in his head until he couldn't think anymore. Everywhere he looked he saw and heard baseball, even when it wasn't mentioned. Even the simplest words and phrases seemed to have a curve to them.

When he was well enough, he started venturing out and meeting people. Often those he met would offer condolences on the loss of his career, and Ricardo wished that he hadn't left seclusion. But one day he was kicking a few stray pebbles as he walked down the strip when he ran into an old classmate. The strip hadn't changed much, except that now there was a second Baptist church at the end of the street.

Ricardo spoke with Anne for quite some time before he realized that she didn't follow sports or local gossip. She had no idea what had happened to him. The conversation was refreshing. He asked her questions about her life to get his mind off his own, and she was glad to talk. She worked as a high school teacher a few counties away, and she mentioned that the school needed a baseball coach.

Ricardo drove to the school a few days later. He decided to take the job when it was offered, thinking that if he could somehow still be connected to the game that it might help him to get through his misery. It was when he stepped onto the field and began working with the young players that he finally understood. When he saw how the players improved with his suggestions, he began to feel a purpose again. He did love the game, and while the game itself had no affection, his students had more than enough to compensate.

All of Ricardo's life up until this point, he'd been pursuing the dream of fame. But that wasn't the desire of his heart. What he really wanted was admiration. Ricardo thought that these two were the same thing, but they aren't. Fame is capricious, at best. Admiration for talent will perish with a career. Maura gave him the kind of admiration that he craved, but he couldn't recognize it. She had supported Ricardo's career because she loved him, not his ability.

What Ricardo needed most was the thing that he had pushed aside in order to reach the goal that he wanted to achieve. It wasn't until his career suddenly halted like a fastball making contact with a limp bat that Ricardo honestly looked into his own heart. Then he understood what he really needed. He needed to give something of himself in order to achieve the kind of relationships that would benefit him in the long term.

You can ask anyone he coached. Those who failed to learn from Ricardo can only blame themselves for ignoring his lessons. The things his players learned went beyond the game and improved their lives. He taught those players priceless lessons. For example, one time when the outfielders weren't paying attention to the exercises he was doing with the infielders, Ricardo suddenly hit fifteen balls over the fence in different directions, and he told the outfielders to go retrieve them all. Ricardo could still hit well and it took over thirty minutes for those players to round up every ball. When they breathlessly returned with the balls, Ricardo spoke to them patiently.

"You always back up the infielders. That's your job. You prevent a single from turning into a double or a double turning into a triple. You prevent runs from scoring when you're right where you're needed when you're needed. If you can't do this, then you might as well not be on the team at all. Poor timing is as bad as no timing. And timing is everything. That goes for everything on and off the field.

You might quit the game and never play baseball again, but never forget what I just told you. Timing is everything. You lose your timing and you screw up your game. Or your life."

A baseball field is its own universe. The ball is the center of everything there. Every motion, every action, every play revolves around that orb. There are two forces that work in opposition to win the game: one that tries to maintain the fluidity of the ball's motion and the other that works to kill it. The team at bat wants the ball to remain in motion while runs are scored. The team on the field wants to prevent that motion until it's their turn at bat. The only way to achieve that goal is through teamwork.

Life can be like the game. For example, Ricardo learned that he had no concept of timing or teamwork when it came to love. He lost Maura because of it. He needed her, but he couldn't recognize it because he wasn't focused. In baseball, that's like taking your eye off the ball. The goal of baseball is to work as a team, not to be a star. Teams, not individuals, win games. If you have a group of magnificent players but they don't know how to work together, the team will fail. Ricardo learned this about base ball early, but he learned this about life too late.

"It still doesn't tell me why you woke me up," I remark during the long pause of contentment following the conclusion of the story. The moon gazes at me with a special warmth in the light irradiating from his eyes.

"When I speak, I whisper truth. This is why you cannot distinguish the difference between your voice and mine: because I am telling you what you already know and what your heart recognizes as familiar. I speak the truth that you mortals dare not speak to yourselves." As he gazes down at me, he deluges my face with cascades of his iridescent light. I close my eyes as the light washes over me. The feeling is overwhelming to the senses. When the moon shines favor, he does it with fullness, and there have been times when I could hardly stand because of the weight of his affection. When I open my eyes and smile again, he continues speaking, "This is why I speak in dreams: because it is the only place where I can speak openly to a person's heart. Dreams are the only place where you humans are truly honest with yourselves. And this is the primary reason people seldom share their dreams with one another." He smiles again at me, and I understand completely.

"You knew that I wanted to talk with you," I remark with admiration. I watch the gentle rays of light flood from his eyes as he gazes down at my face. He knows my heart, and I am not afraid of him.

Chapter
Five
Moonbeams and Magic

The moon can do magic. He can put a spell on hair to make it grow thicker and faster. If you happen to be bald, then you should be more cautious. You may have offended the moon at one time. He's not often forgiving, so there's scant hope that your hair will return.

He often plays tricks and casts spells on people. This is how he amuses himself when he's in one of his roguish moods.

When he's in his most mischievous moments, the moon sometimes plays with his moonbeams. Moonlight is powerful stuff. He can transform the appearance of anything with moonlight. You might think that you see a maple tree. Then you glance at the tree another time, and it's become a dragon. You quickly look again, and it's a simple maple tree once more. The moon is full of this mischief.

"Have you no conscience?" I ask one evening when the weather is particularly warm and the moon exceptionally puckish. He's in his waning crescent phase. There is something about this phase that makes him especially playful. Perhaps he knows that he will soon be in the New Moon phase and virtually invisible to us mortals below. Whatever the reason, he's something of a rascal.

He laughs at my remark, and I watch huge clouds of sparkling dust billow forth from each chuckle. His laugh is rhythmic, as so many of his behaviors are.

I tell him that his game is a cruel one, but he discounts my concern. "It is mostly drunks that I fool in this manner. If they didn't enjoy losing control of their perceptions, they wouldn't indulge in alcohol so much." Having never been given to drink, I had no answer for him. "However," he continues, "There are some tricks that do more good than harm."

"I don't see how…"

"Let me explain," and here he began another story.

Some people say houses have souls. Maybe the soul of the house is that part of the building's identity that is formed by the characteristics of the owner. Or perhaps it's the lingering spirit of the events that have taken place within the building. In either case, a house is more than a container for human events: each one has an atmosphere of its own. There is a presence of character that belongs uniquely to each dwelling place that transcends the scope of current occupants. The Hunter mansion was like this. Although few people had ever stepped inside, the house radiated a presence of mystery. The mansion was closed up most of the time, and even when it was occupied, no one assumed that the current dweller was human. Everyone who looked at the house knew that it must have at least one ghost, and more likely several of them.

The noises didn't help the mansion's reputation. The majority of locals had only heard rumors of the unearthly sounds, but those whose ears experienced the ghostly noises described them as "inhuman" or "eerie."

"The ghost travels through sound waves and tries to enter your soul by boring through your eardrum and into your body," the town pharmacist once told a young boy who was talking about the house with his friends.

"Ghosts don't take over people," the dark-haired boy responded cautiously, his eyes filling with apprehension.

"This one does, and there's no medicine that will cure you if it happens. And if the ghost gets inside you, it will take you out of this world, and we'll find your body floating in the river. Don't play anywhere near that house, and keep your windows closed at night."

As much as people feared the noises and the potential specters, it was stories like this one that drew some people toward the mansion. Most of these were teenage boys looking to impress a date. In fact, it was a popular pastime in this particular rural Midwestern town to sit in the field opposite the house late at night among the rows of wheat, drinking whatever you could sneak out of your parents' liquor cabinet and watch the mansion for signs of ghostly activity. The stalks of wheat provided a natural veil between the intoxicated mortals and whatever supernatural force existed just beyond the edge of the field in that house. There was something about sitting upon the solid, rich earth that made observers feel protected from the ghostlike presence of the mansion.

Josh and his friends did this often. It started when they were in their junior year of high school. By the fall of their senior year, it was a Friday night ritual. It was the boys' method of unwinding after a football game and the girls were there only to be with the boys from the team. There were four of them in all. Five, if you count Josh's dog, Corby. The boys would start the evening by trying to scare the girls with stories. Sometimes they'd stay long enough to watch the legendary old woman arrive at the house in a taxi and watch her go inside, wondering if she was mortal or a ghost. Each time they saw her withered form moving slowly through the darkness, the boys felt chills and the girls felt faint.

No one knew the full story behind the house. As far as anyone could tell, it was vacant during the week. But late on Friday nights, Mrs. Hunter would arrive. She never went into town and never went outside. The only time any-one saw her frail, slightly crumpled figure was as she made her way between the house and taxi. No one knew the taxi driver or where he came from. Most people assumed that the cab either came from a location very far away or that it came from the grave. There were as many stories about the taxi as there were about Mrs. Hunter. The only thing any-one knew for certain was her name. It was hand painted on the mailbox in bold red letters.

On this particular evening, as the warm early autumn breeze gently rustled the strands of wheat, Josh and Brandon told the girls how Mrs. Hunter had actually died in a gruesome traffic accident while riding in a taxi cab on a Friday evening years ago and her ghost was still trying to make its way home.

"Watch her feet when she gets here," Josh insisted, "they don't even touch the ground when she gets out of the cab. She just kind of floats and leaves a trickle of blood on the ground beneath her. She bled to death in the accident, you know."

"You're lying," Missy protested with a giggle. She quickly looked down and took a sip of flat beer. Then she turned her attention away from the boys and their story to watch the wheat move, wondering if it was the wind or her mind playing tricks on her.

"No, really." Brandon spoke in earnest, "I walked up to the house last Saturday, and there was a trail of blood go-ing from the drive to the front door. I saw it with my own eyes." He gestured clumsily in front of his face, as if to conjure up the scene and validate the contents of his story.

"You're both liars." Alice tried to sound convinced, but the boys knew they were gaining the advantage, and Brandon decided that tonight he would try to kiss Missy when she fell into his arms. At least he hoped that she would fall close enough to him so that he could catch her.

"You wish we were lying. Just wait and see. The old lady will get here soon. Try not to scream when you see that she's not walking on two legs like the rest of us."

So they waited. It was lucky for them that they didn't have much beer to drink that night. They thought they were drinking for courage or to relax, but it only dulled their perceptions and made it harder for them to see things clearly. To this day these four teenagers aren't sure exactly what they saw or what happened.

There was a bright shimmer of moonlight reflecting off the top of the car that pulled up the long driveway and stopped directly in front of the mansion. The car looked and smelled tangible with exhaust fumes that reeked of burned gasoline. The onlookers studied the side of the cab, which appeared to be brown with a bluish dusting across the top where the dim light bounced off the metal. Brandon tried to read the dark lettering on the side of the cab, but only the word "Taxi" was clear enough for him to distinguish. The immense trees behind the house stood up like giant claws against the sky and cast obscure shadows over the car, making it impossible to see anyone inside and giving the cab the appearance of having a phantom driver. It seemed as if nothing was happening for a long time, and then there was a sudden red glow like a solitary demonic eye burning in the darkness of the cab's interior. As the glowing eye dissipated into blackness, the kids relaxed. It was only the end of a lighted cigarette.

Then the top of Mrs. Hunter's gray head was visible just above the roof of the car. Her long hair was swept up into a bun that bulged with the volume of tresses. A few loose strands swayed in the wind and waved erratically as she turned to ascend the steps into the house.

None of the kids could see the old woman's feet because she got out of the taxi on the side closest to the house. Mrs. Hunter was so tiny that only her hair was visible from behind the car. The kids were convinced, however, that she was floating. Missy let out a faint, but shrill scream. She didn't swoon the way Brandon had hoped, and he was beginning to feel discouraged when the old woman hesitated on the steps of the house and stood with her back toward the field where the kids were hiding. She slowly pivoted on her foot and turned around just as the taxi was leaving. The way her unfocused eyes stared out in front of her and her pointy chin remained in line with her torso made the movement seem unnatural. She paused as she tried to look toward the dark field. The sound of pebbles crunching underneath the wheels of the taxi grew faint until the taxi disappeared altogether. For more than a minute, Mrs. Hunter gazed blankly into the shadowy silence, and the teenagers grew more uncomfortable in her presence. Each of the four kids was convinced that the old woman was staring directly at him or her when she suddenly spoke.

"Missy, is that you?" she called out loudly. There was no way she could have known that Missy was in the wheat field. At least, no earthly way. She had never even met Missy, let alone heard that a girl named Missy existed. But she spoke again and this time with more determination.

"Missy, come here. I need you to help me find my

Thomas." Her voice cracked as she spoke in a feeble, but stern manner.

"Who's Thomas?" Brandon whispered to Missy after a period of uneasy silence.

"How should I know?" she replied defensively.

"She's asking you to help her find him."

"That doesn't mean that I already know who he is. Maybe he's another ghost."

"What's your grandfather's name?" Brandon asked.

"My grandpa has nothing to do with this!"

"But what's his name?"

"Ed."

"Did he have a brother?"

"You're not making sense. Shut up!"

Corby let out a fragrant belch of the stew that Josh had earlier slipped to him from the dinner table. Josh was like a vending machine, dispensing food to his companion every time Corby poked Josh on the leg, using his nose like a battering ram to obtain a treat. Josh giggled as he smelled the aroma of beef and garlic. The dog looked nearly repentant for a moment as his eyes searched the faces around him. Then the old woman spoke again.

"Missy, I can hear you." The old woman cupped her bony hands around her mouth as she spoke. Her voice was high and frail sounding, and as she tried to project the volume, the tone crackled.

"This is creepy." Alice's voice trembled as she spoke. "If she wants Missy, let's give her Missy before she takes the rest of us to who-knows-where."

"The house may be a gateway to hell," Josh reasoned aloud. As he finished speaking, Corby began a low growl in the direction of the old woman. This normally gentle dog's eyes were filled with a mixture of hostility and defensiveness, and it further unnerved the kids. "I don't like this," Josh announced quietly. "Dogs have a sixth sense, and Corby is a very good judge of character. If my dog doesn't like someone, then they must be a cat, a very bad person or a ghost."

Before anyone could respond to the remark, Corby's upper lip curled tightly as his fangs emerged. The girls had never seen Corby turn on anyone, and this further unnerved them. As if he could sense the girls' increasing fear, Corby deepened the growl directed at the old lady's dark silhouette. He pointed his tail straight back as his fluffy white body stood poised to lurch forward. Then a gust of warm air suddenly rushed past and agitated the surrounding foliage of the nearby trees. Suddenly it was as if the old lady rose off the ground and began hovering in place, as if she could swoosh down upon all of them in a matter of seconds. The autumn wind tossed the loose strands of her hair wildly in different directions as the white chiffon scarf around her neck flapped angrily.

On impulse the kids bolted from their hiding place and quickly ran away from the spinster and the house. When the old woman saw the kids running, she shouted such archaic expletives that they were convinced she was placing a curse upon all of them.

It's unfortunate for Brandon that he was in love with Missy, or maybe he would have had a little sense. The next day when Missy begged him to go back to the house and investigate why the old woman wanted her, Brandon agreed to do it without thinking and also volunteered his best friend to go with him.

"You had no right to tell her that I would do this," Josh complained as he stroked the back of Corby's neck.

"Come on. She's scared of the old bat. You and I

know she's just a creepy old lady." While Brandon was attempting to sound confident, his voice didn't match the assurance of his words. Still he continued, "We'll go up to the house, bring back some sort of proof that we were there, and we'll look like heroes to the girls."

"The old bat is a little too creepy. Not even Missy's parents knew where she was, and Mrs. Hunter said her name, like she just knew that Missy was there." Corby raised his paw and tenderly placed it upon Josh's knee. Josh acknowledged the gesture by placing his free hand on the top of the dog's paw. Then Corby melted to the floor, resting his head in Josh's lap and exposing his stomach to Josh with an appealing gaze. Josh vigorously rubbed the dog's belly.

"Missy won't be with us, and Mrs. Hunter wasn't interested in anyone else," Brandon insisted. "Just bring Corby along. That crazy old lady can't get past your dog."

"What if something happens to Corby?" Josh protested. He gazed down at his dog resting like a wet noodle on top of him. Corby moaned in ecstasy as Josh's hands traced repetitive patterns through the dog's soft coat.

"You said he had a sixth sense. He'll warn us if any

thing weird is happening, and we'll get away just like we did last night. We can go up along the river to the back of the house. That senile lady won't even know we're there." Brandon did a wonderful job of convincing himself as he spoke. While Josh had little faith in Brandon, he was confident in Corby and agreed to go. In a way, Josh wanted to return to the mansion so that he could convince himself that he had seen nothing out of the ordinary the night before. He still wasn't sure what he had seen and what he had imagined.

When Brandon and Josh set out for the Hunter mansion with Corby, they took the path along the river, which led up through the woods to the back side of the old house. The tree roots along the riverbank were thick and obtrusive. The gnarly masses took on spooky manifestations within the boys' minds. The closer the boys came to the house, the thicker the trees became, and the less they saw of the moon. Dense shadows took on many different forms from the ghostly to the absurd. The path became less clear, and the two boys became unsure of their steps. They slowed to a cautious pace, occasionally stopping with a jerk when the river made a noise that was slightly out of character. The wind was blowing a bit harder, and every gust carried with it a hint of the supernatural. Josh put his hand on Corby's neck as they neared the back of the house. Corby showed no sign of apprehension and was playfully enjoying the moonlit walk, stopping occasionally to press his nose high in the air to search the woodsy scent for information on his surroundings.

"Missy will never know if you went up to the house or not," Josh whispered to his friend.

Then they heard the legendary noise that so few had heard and so many found indescribable. It was the old woman, but the sound was unrecognizable as human. It was more of a staggering moan than a cry, and there was something desperate about it. The boys didn't know exactly where she was when they stopped walking, but she was close. They heard her faint, crackling moan as if it was coming directly out of the tree they were standing against. The old woman may have been crying, because her voice continually broke as she tried to speak out in elongated tones.

"Thomas." The wind carried her breathy call to the boys' ears. They both took a step backward as a light snapped on. The old lady's white gown pressed against her tiny body in the wind and made her frail structure look skeletal. Her face glowed in the light, but her eyes were dark and hollow looking without discernible pupils. Neither boy could see anything that resembled the presence of feet, so they both took off running toward town with Corby following. When they had gone a few hundred feet, Corby suddenly turned around with a loud growl and took off back in the direction of the Hunter Mansion. Josh paused for a moment, wondering which way to go. He could chase his dog and run toward the ghostly image, or continue in his escape. Josh decided to follow Brandon, who was running faster than he ever did on the football field. Josh was certain that Corby could look after himself.

But Corby didn't come home that night. Monday morning didn't bring him home, either, and Josh didn't want to go to school, but his mother insisted that Corby was probably out with a girlfriend and would return by nightfall. She knew that the dog had never gone out by himself for more than an hour before and that Corby was usually wherever Josh was. Corby was practically welded to Josh's side. Even when Josh was at school, Corby waited near the cherry tree just outside the science room window so that he could walk home with Josh.

Three days after Corby had disappeared, Josh's mother admitted that the dog must be lost, and Josh started posting signs around town. Josh was angry with his mother for not allowing him to look for Corby immediately after the dog vanished, but he was also angry with himself for not going after Corby that night by the river.

Every morning when Josh woke up, he ignored the scent of breakfast cooking and went outside in his pajamas to see if Corby was on the porch. Josh usually left for school without eating, no matter how many of his favorites foods his mother had prepared. His only appetite was to see his dog again.

A month went by with no sign of Corby. Josh became more depressed and stopped spending time with his friends on the weekends. It wasn't the same. He wasn't even curious about the old woman and whether she was a ghost. Besides, he had decided that if she was anything at all, she was a witch who had taken his dog from him. Josh wondered if that old woman had lured Corby there for some purpose of black magic or devilish ritual. Or maybe she really was a ghost and had taken control of Corby by entering his soul through his eardrum, just like the rumor. After all, dogs have better hearing, and a sensitive eardrum may be just what the ghost needed for easy entry into a mortal's body. Josh spent hours speculating on such things.

Josh missed Corby so much that he couldn't do much of anything. Even watching TV seemed to take too much energy. Josh lost so much weight that the coach pulled him from the starting lineup, but Josh didn't care. He quit going to practice. Instead of sleeping, he stared at his bedroom walls until he knew that his parents had gone to bed. Then he'd put on his shoes and go out walking in search of Corby. The first few nights, he stayed close to home as he strolled past neighboring farms. Then his walks strayed toward the mansion. Once or twice Josh thought he heard the old woman calling, and he quickly went home, half desiring to surrender his mortal body to her if it meant that he'd be with Corby again.

One night as he strayed toward the mansion, he began to hear Mrs. Hunter's desperate call again. It was that same unearthly moan crying out something that sounded like,

"I'm lost! I'm lost!" She was calling in that same breathy, whimpering tone she had used the night Corby disappeared, and it stirred something inside Josh. In his own desperation, he wondered if Corby was somehow using the specter to call to him. Josh walked faster and even though his fear increased with each step he soon found himself running toward the sound of the old woman's voice. As he neared the house, he spotted the beam of her flashlight moving around and casting shadows on the dead leaves. Josh stopped running but continued moving determinedly toward her, as if drawn by an unseen force. As her ghostly figure moved languidly across the path, Josh quickly glanced down to see that she had feet. They were bony and fragile looking, wrapped in velvet slippers that shimmered in the moonlight, but they were real feet, and she was standing on them. Then he noticed that she was talking to herself or reciting an incantation of some sort. She spoke quickly and in low tones that Josh couldn't hear until she suddenly looked up again and broke out in that same cry. Her moaning was light, eerie and constant. As she turned to face Josh, he heard her clearly call out, "Thomas!" She wasn't crying out because she was lost.

She was calling for Thomas again.

"Who?" Josh demanded loudly, but she didn't hear him or see him. She started talking to herself once again, and Josh strained to hear what sort of spell she was casting in the midnight air. She waved the flashlight around as she spoke, and Josh started to recognize individual words among the low mumbling sounds.

"More evil … mischief … I'll be dead …" Josh was certain that he heard her say these words as the beam of light she was holding darted erratically across the ground. Josh's determination suddenly left him, and he froze. She darted erratically in circles, as if in some hellish dance that caused her to reach toward the earth. Josh wondered if the grave was attempting to pull her back into the soil and this tarantella was a result of her resistance, but then she stopped and cursed loudly.

"Thomas, you bastard cat! I've had enough of your wanderings and chasing strays. That Missy is nothing but a slut who would starve to death if I didn't leave her food. Now you can both die of hunger for all I care. You ungrateful cats!" She continued to curse as she snapped off the flashlight and stomped her way back through the forest to ward the mansion, looking more real than she ever had. Josh watched the shadow of a large calico moving stealthily away, as it glanced back at the old woman with an expression of contempt.

"So, you're Thomas," Josh whispered more to himself than to the cat. At the sound of his name, Thomas glanced at Josh in annoyance and then continued on his way.

Now Josh knew why Corby took off in such a rush. There was a mischievous cat who liked to sneak out of the mansion and prowl in the woods. The night Corby disappeared, he was chasing cats.

Josh kept this information to himself, still wondering if the woman was human or ghostly. On most days he thought she was real and listened to any other stories about her with concealed amusement. But since Corby hadn't returned, there was a part of Josh that continued to wonder if the old woman was an occultist or involved in some other evil practice. Some unseen force had kept a 40-pound, physically fit dog from coming back to him. Josh continued to take walks late at night when his parents thought he was asleep.

It was on one of these late night wanderings that he found the dog. The animal was covered with scratches and wounds as he slept curled up on the side of the road, the moonlight casting a bluish glow on his white coat. His face was mangled beyond recognition, but when Josh called out "Corby!" the dog looked up at him with a helpless, exhausted expression. Tears streamed down Josh's face as he scooped up the dog in both of his arms and carried the heavy, limp body home.

The veterinarian examined the dog the next day, awed that the canine was still alive after whatever trauma had caused such extensive wounds. "Maybe a mountain lion," the vet suggested as he treated the lacerations on the dog's face. Dr. Williams gave Josh explicit instructions on nursing the animal, but anyone could see that the doctor wasn't confident the dog would live. Josh carefully tended to his injured pal. He set up a comfortable sleeping place inside his bedroom for the animal to be near him. He even slept on the floor next to the dog the first few nights. Josh was convinced that he loved his friend enough to save him. Josh stroked the animal's neck as he slowly squirted water down his throat with a syringe to prevent dehydration. For several days Josh repeated this procedure because the dog was too weak to stand up and drink on his own. Josh administered medication to prevent infection, and he cleaned and dressed his friend's wounds twice a day.

Despite the vet's dismal prognosis and much to everyone's surprise, the dog began to get well. Maybe it was all the attention that Josh showered on it. Perhaps there is a healing power in the act of loving; the knowledge that a human companion was so devoted to the animal strengthened his efforts to survive and recover. Josh was so elated the first time that the dog stood up and began to eat that Josh nearly cried.

While Josh was thrilled about the animal's recovery, he could not escape the feeling that something was wrong. As the wounds on his pet's face healed, Josh began to notice things that weren't the same about him. There were patches of fur that were cream colored instead of pure white. The dog acted a little differently also. He was more skittish about noise especially thunder, which had never bothered Corby before.

"He's spent some time outside in the elements. That could make him nervous about sounds," Dr. Williams explained as he examined the dog. "And he's had scarring. He may never look exactly the same after what's he's been though," the vet assured Josh. "It's just like your hair changing with age. It happens with dogs also. Age or trauma can affect the way they look."

"Are you sure that something else couldn't cause the change?"

"Like what?"

Josh hesitated. He felt foolish suggesting it, but the other kids at school were convinced. Dr. Williams waited patiently for Josh to explain, and so he finally did.

"Some people think that maybe the old witch did this."

"Witch?" Dr. Williams looked confused.

"Corby got lost near the Hunter mansion," Josh explained. "And I found him not too far from there, too. Some people think that the witch put a spell on him or tried to sacrifice him."

Dr. Williams laughed.

"That's just superstition," he said. "There's no witch at that mansion. It's stuff like what happened to poor Corby here that spreads those rumors. But there's no truth in it."

"Have you ever seen her? That old lady, I mean. Have you ever gotten a good look at her?"

"Not really."

"No one in this town has. Don't you think that's a little odd?"

"I can't say that's exactly normal, but that doesn't make her a witch. I've never seen her up close, but I've spoken with her on the phone once or twice. She takes in stray cats, and she's called me a few times when they wouldn't come home before Sunday night when she had to drive back to Chicago. She asked me to find someone to take care of the cats during the week by leaving them food and fresh water on the porch. She paid my assistant generously for doing the favor. She seemed perfectly normal."

"But why don't' we ever see her? She never goes into town."

"I don't know," Dr. Williams shrugged. "That house sits outside of town, and not too many people ever knew what went on there even when Mrs. Hunter didn't own it. All I know is that she inherited the house and only spends two days a week in it. There's nothing wrong with some one from the city wanting quiet for a couple of days now and then. I don't see how being a recluse makes her a witch. You're letting your imagination run away with you. Besides, Corby's face was scratched by something with claws. Those wounds weren't made by a person. Another animal attacked your dog, and he's very lucky to be alive. Let's just be thankful for that and stop worrying about witches. There is nothing wrong with your dog now, and that's all that matters." Dr. Williams spoke convincingly, but there was something about the way that he looked at Corby as he finished speaking that left Josh feeling confused. "Unless..." Dr. Williams thoughtfully stared at the dog and then carried him over to the scale to weigh the animal. When he was finished, he checked the weight with the dog's medical record. "The exact same weight as he was before he was lost the same weight to the pound. I would say that for all practical purposes that your dog is back to normal."

Josh would have believed it, but in his heart he knew that something was different. After a few more weeks passed, Josh decided that it didn't matter what had changed about his dog or why. He knew that he loved the animal and would have given his own life to save him if it had come to that. Every afternoon when Josh got home from school, the two sat out on the porch together, as long as it wasn't thundering. Josh finished his homework there or talked with Brandon as the dog appealed to the girls for attention.

"Corby, you flirt!" Missy exclaimed as Corby gingerly licked her knee. Then she turned to Brandon, "He's as bad as you."

"No one is as bad as Brandon," Alice replied in a matter-of-fact voice. "Taking us over to that mansion and scaring us just to get his arms around you, Missy."

"We haven't been back there," Brandon informed Josh quietly.

"I went back, but not with you," Josh replied calmly. "That's where I found Corby." At the mention of his name, the dog sat upright. "That's right. I'm talking about you," Josh teased the animal, but the canine walked away from his master and stood attentively, looking down at the front lawn, his white plumed tail curled up and held high. It was a sign that he was alert. The group followed the dog's stare down the lawn to view what looked like his mirror image. Corby was standing on the porch, but he also seemed to be standing on the front lawn, staring back.

Josh let out a gasp as he saw the two dogs look each other over. They were like twins or clones. Both dogs were pure white with subtle cream-colored markings in nearly the same places. They were the same height, width, length, and physical build. Their noses and eyes had the same shapes and they both held their ears up in nearly the same position, the left one slightly lower than the right.

"Corby?" Josh called the name out loud and both dogs turned to look at him expectantly.

"Have we been drinking?" Alice asked cautiously, "Because I think I'm seeing double."

"Witchcraft!" Missy exclaimed.

"Corby?" Josh called again and both dogs dashed to his side. The confusion was dizzying. Josh held each dog's face in his hands and stared in the eyes, but he wasn't sure what he saw. Both dogs looked back at him with affection and recognition. It was as if they both knew and loved him. Then Josh looked at the dog he had nursed back to health and understood. He also felt the pleasure of relief in finally seeing the truth of his situation.

"You're not Corby." He said aloud to the dog. "You look a lot like Corby and you act a lot like him. Maybe you had the same parents, but you aren't him."

"He even fooled me," Dr. Williams said as he walked up to the porch and greeted the kids. "They do look like twins. They're about the same age and weight."

"Did you bring him here? Where did you find him?" Josh asked, looking around for Dr. Williams' deep blue truck until he spotted it parked on the road.

"I drove him here, but I didn't find him," Dr. Williams smiled to himself. "It's kind of funny, really." He put both his hands in his pockets as he continued to grin.

"Let us in on the joke," Missy insisted.

"He's been staying with Mrs. Hunter. She found him the night Corby ran away, and I have to say Corby has been so loved and well fed that I don't think it ever occurred to Corby that he should have gone home. Mrs. Hunter called me yesterday and told me she had taken in a stray dog but that she couldn't keep him anymore since she spent more time in Chicago than here in the country. She's been taking Corby to Chicago with her, but Corby doesn't seem to like it there. Mrs. Hunter wanted to know if I could find him a good home."

"I can't believe she's not a ghost, after all," Missy mumbled in disbelief.

"I can't believe Josh didn't have tags on his dog," Dr. Williams countered. "You kids worked yourselves up over something that didn't exist. You created worries and fears, and the whole time you were agonizing over Corby, he was filling his belly with steak and fries. The only bad thing that woman did was to spoil Corby's diet."

"We thought we were really brave by sneaking up on a ghost," Brandon said. "Now we're just a couple of idiots who only fooled ourselves." He folded his arms as he thought about the situation, wondering how he looked to Missy in light of all this.

"I fooled myself more than any of us," Josh mused out loud, "Now that Corby is here, I can see that I wanted him so much that I convinced myself I had found him." Josh put one hand on each of the dogs' necks and stroked them both fondly.

"What are you going to do with the other dog?" Dr. Williams suddenly asked.

"Keep him," Josh announced as he shrugged. "He's

very lucky that I was out looking for Corby and found him when I did, so I'll call him Lucky."

But Josh couldn't escape feeling that, in the end, he was luckiest of all of them.

"While many situations work themselves out in the end, the careless invite trouble by their very attitude," the moon continues. "Youth is often most careless, and fate should never be trusted to leave anyone alone. Good or bad." He pauses to blink, and as he does so, moonbeams rain down in glimmering sheaths upon two lovers nearby. A few rays continue to trickle in sparkling drips from his lashes. "Caution can never be underrated." His smile is no longer mischievous as he continues to shower the lovers with his magical light.

Chapter
Six
Waxing and Waning

The moon doesn't understand the fascination that humans have with gold. "How does it feel to hold diamonds?" he asks. "Or gold? People seem to love gold. What about currency? Does that have a special texture? What do these things contain that make humans want them in their hands?" I tell him that it's better to feel moonbeams caressing my bare skin. While he is clearly pleased by the compliment, he still doesn't understand. "Then why do humans strive so much for currency? Has anyone ever murdered another human being to feel the touch of a moonbeam?"

"Moonbeams are free," I point out.

"But not less precious. One has only to walk outside at night to feel moonbeams. But one must toil for gold. Perhaps if I made people work for my gifts they would be better appreciated."

"Perhaps," I agree half-heartedly. He cannot easily understand. He has no need of money or status. He is certainly full of pride. But he is also unique and without need to prove himself: he's the only moon that Earth has. He knows nothing of social status; he lacks any competition for position. He has never known want; his needs are few. He has never hungered for anything, not even admiration.

"The true value of a gift is not in the cost," he remarks sorrowfully. "But humans don't know how to measure real worth, and so they resort to price tags. And what is the exact value of the money you seek to gain? Only that which you people decide. It's an arbitrary manner in which to live." He sighs, and when he does so, a swirling ray of mercury-like droplets shimmer through the night sky for that moment. His breath is powerful and magnificent. "I've watched generations who fail to learn this lesson. It's heart-breaking to watch. Take this story about a gift. Some of these events happened only across town from you." He inhales deeply as he prepares to narrate. Then he slowly but powerfully exhales that beautiful stream of breath.

This story begins early in the last century, during the time of silent films. During this period, there was a very famous film star whose name was commonly known in just about any American household. She was a pretty thing, and the entire country was enamored of her charm, especially her large, round eyes. They were the color of honey, but few people knew this, as her films were in black and white. This film star, whom we shall call Vanessa, was all the rage. Women all over the country imitated her hairstyle, clothes, and even her mannerisms. Men from everywhere from all over the world-- sent her marriage proposals and gifts. One gift she received was a ring. The giver wrote her a long passionate letter begging her to wear the ring but asking nothing more. He told her that the ring was moonstone, to match her beauty, which he declared was beyond earthly splendor. But the ring was in truth an opal, and quite an exquisite one. The setting was a gold filigree of delicate intricacy. Vanessa liked the look of fire within the stone and she took to wearing it regularly. The ring was immediately noticed, and gossip circulated through the newspapers. Columnists speculated who had given her the ring and what it meant. Every week for two years there was a new story about Vanessa, and the ring was always mentioned and speculated upon in some manner. Usually it was supposed that the ring was an engagement present. But, like her movies, Vanessa was silent. She liked the mystery, and the publicity only increased her popularity.

The ring even incited jealousy from a number of her lovers, each of whom tried to provide her with a ring that she would prefer more than this mysterious opal. But every one of them failed, and she continued to wear the ring, although she had never met the giver. Whenever someone asked her who had given her the ring, Vanessa would reply coolly, "Why, this is a moonstone. So the moon must have given it to me."

About ten years passed in this manner. Vanessa was at the height of her popularity, and every leading man in Hollywood sought her affection. Then there was a tumultuous change in the film industry: talkies arrived. While Vanessa had been the perfect leading lady of silent films, her voice was less than heavenly. Her speaking tone was nasal, and she had an accent that sounded more like a trash collector from South Boston than a starlet. The studio hired numerous voice coaches for her, but when her first talking picture came out, the public turned away. The sweetheart who appeared so perfect was suddenly too human. She never made another film. Her popularity plummeted, and after a few years she was pawning everything she owned to buy food. Finally, she pawned the ring to a jeweler who saw the exquisiteness of the stone, the fineness of the setting, and the fact that it had belonged to such a famous owner. He expected to make a nice profit on the ring. He gave Vanessa $500 for it, which was a lot of money at the time. But shortly after Vanessa died in poverty two years later, the jeweler auctioned the ring for $7,800.

A very successful businessman attended the auction, looking for curiosities. He bought the ring as a Christmas present for his wife. The wife, whom I shall not name because she is quite well known in this town, wore the ring intermittently for nearly twenty years. She was not as captivated by the ring as her husband, so she wore the ring mostly to please him. She often wore the ring when attending charity dinners or when she went to fund-raising events. It was beautiful but not nearly as ostentatious as diamonds, and because of this she thought it perfect for such functions. The ring got plenty of notice at these events. The stone caught the evening light when she danced, or produced a fiery glow under candlelight. The husband enjoyed the attention the ring brought, and time after time he retold the story of the auction and about how he had cleverly outbid his competitors. While the listeners became tired of the husband's story, they did not tire of admiring the ring.

There were times when this husband and wife would have dinner alone; just the two of them in that grand house at the top of Main Street. The cook would prepare an elaborate meal and then leave for the evening. On these intimate occasions the husband would ask his wife to wear the ring so that he could admire it on her lovely hand.

"What else should I wear?" she would ask every time.

"Who cares what else?" and there was always mischief in his voice when he said this.

Over the course of twenty years the wealthy socialite remained quite beautiful. Her hair was still blond, but slightly darker. Her eyes were still a clear blue that reflected every light, and perhaps made some of their own when the room was too dim. Even though she had aged some, she was still very striking, even by celestial standards. So no one could explain why her husband had the affair. I doubt that even the husband knew why he did it. This is one of those things that even I can't explain, but it happened and the wife was quite hurt over it all. When the husband offered no apology, other than saying something to the effect of "Boys will be boys, and men will be men" she became angry. She stewed silently until the next holiday, when she gave the opal ring to her housekeeper as a Christmas gift. You see, the wife viewed the ring as the most valuable thing that her husband had given her, and this was her method of getting even.

When the husband learned what his wife had done with the ring, he was furious. He raved for days while the wife tried to disguise her satisfaction. He called her crazy and howled scathing names at her. Sometimes he would walk into the room where she was writing a letter or working, and he'd tear the small pair of spectacles from his face as if about to make a point. But then he'd re-place his glasses and leave the room, sweeping his anger along with him. Finally, he confronted her aloud.

"You gave away that ring like it was nothing. Nothing!   What you've done is insane. Hannah doesn't know the value of such a thing. You've cast pearls before swine."

"And so have you," was the quiet reply that silenced him permanently on the subject.

Hannah was a hard-working woman and very grateful for the generous gift. She didn't own any jewelry except for the plain gold wedding band that her husband had given her. Hannah didn't know the exact value of the ring, but her mistress had explained the identity of the original owner and told Hannah that the ring was valuable because of its history. Hannah didn't have much money, but she did have three children who were almost grown at the time. The thought of selling the ring in order to pay for a good education for at least one of the children was too tempting for her. So, like the original owner, Hannah took the ring to a jeweler to sell it.

The jeweler scrutinized the ring under his eyepiece.

"It looks like there's a fissure," he remarked in a skep-

tical voice. Hannah didn't know what a fissure was. She re-
mained silent. "The setting is scratched. It's quite old.
Most people want new. And opals are out of fashion now.
Everyone wants sapphires. That's what's in."

"The ring used to belong to a movie star named
Vanessa."

"Vanessa who?"

"A silent film star."

"She couldn't be that famous if you don't remember
her last name." He continued to admire the stone through
his jeweler's glass, but his countenance was stoic. Hannah
watched his thin lips as he set his mouth into an expres-
sionless position.

"The ring is supposed to be valuable." At this remark
the jeweler looked up with undisguised irritation.

"Isn't that my job?" he asked with disdain. He was
well practiced in negotiations of this sort. Hannah was
not. She stroked her pale brown hair with one hand and
then placed the palm of her hand against her chin.

"Yes," she agreed timidly. She stared down at a web of
stains in the carpeting, and she couldn't help but to think
of how simple it would be to remove those stains if some-

one would just take the time. The jeweler took one more look at the ring and decided that the stone was worth keeping, but that the setting must be changed. It was too old fashioned.

"I can give you $5,000 for it." His tone conveyed that he was making a concession, but he already knew of an old client who would pay dearly for such an opal. He expected to double his profit when the ring was reset. Hannah was pleased. This was a large sum for her and half her annual wages. She took the money gladly.

The jeweler put the ring in his safe, but he passed away before he could remove the stone. The jeweler's sons fought over the estate, and the ring was locked up for a number of years. When the fighting was over, the jewelry shop was sold and the proceeds divided among the heirs. The new shop owner knew the retail business but little about jewelry. He put the ring in a display case and later sold it for $250.

The new owner of the ring was a man who collected silent film memorabilia. He recognized the unique ring as either a copy or the original that Vanessa had worn. In either case, it was valuable to him and worth a great deal more than the meager $250 he paid for it. He scurried home with his treasure, and after researching the authenticity, he kept it locked up with his other memorabilia for the rest of his life. No one saw the ring until he decided to auction his collection in preparation for his retirement.

The assortment of memorabilia was extensive, and a prestigious New York firm handled the auction. People from all over the world attended the auction, including a group of three friends who stood near the back and talked quietly among themselves. These men stared at the picture of Vanessa's ring, each with a different expression on his face. The first was determined, the second indifferent, and the third face was clearly skeptical. The indifferent one spoke first.

"So this is why you went to Harvard. This is why you kill yourself working on Wall Street: to spend half your income on a ring."

"Evan, you don't know it's going to cost half my income. It looks like it won't come up for bidding for about another hour," persisted Ben, the gentleman holding the auction guide.

"So let's get out of here and go for coffee. It's

crowded."

"And miss the ring? No way. I can't take the chance."

"No woman is worth that much money," chimed in Jeff. "If she tells you that she's got to have that ring, then she's too high-maintenance."

"You say that about any woman who would inconvenience you," Ben stated with a smug air.

"That would be all of them," Jeff remarked smugly.

"What do you know about 'high-maintenance'? Do you even know what that means?"

"It means that she won't even look at him," Evan replied with a smirk. "If a woman like Jordan was interested in you, Jeff, I think that you'd jump through hoops to keep her."

"If I have to jump through hoops, then she isn't worth keeping," Jeff declared adamantly.

"Now I know why you don't have a girlfriend," Ben remarked with a knowing grin, "Have you ever had one?"

"Funny, Ben. Go ahead and flaunt it. Sure, Jordan's a nice looking woman. I'll give you that. But she knows it. And she knows that you know it and that you're willing to pay the price."

"So?"

"All I'm saying is that a man shouldn't have to prove that he loves a woman by bleeding himself financially to make her happy," Jeff replied firmly.

"You don't know anything about love," Ben sighed with a trace of forced pity in his voice.

"Jeff, you wish that you were able to spend three paychecks to buy a ring for someone like Jordan so that she'd give you the time of day," Evan said, continuing to smirk.

"Why are some women like that?" Jeff asked with some exasperation.

"Because they can be," Ben replied knowingly. "And we just eat it up."

Two hours later, Ben purchased the ring for a little less than thirty thousand dollars. It was most of his savings, but he viewed the ring as an investment. One, I might add, that didn't pay off. Jordan married another man with a much more extensive income. On Jordan's wedding day, Ben took the ring and attached it to the bottom of the pull string on the ceiling fan in his apartment. It was an extremely expensive ornament, but one that taught Ben a priceless lesson. The ring is still there, but hardly anyone notices it except Ben. Sometimes when I'm in my most brilliant phase, he still holds the ring up to my light and watches it glow magnificently.

The moon smiles with the contentment he receives from bringing a story to its conclusion. He glances sideways into space and then winks at one or two of the stars appearing for the night. The stars blink and nod in response, as if they share some infinite knowledge to which we mortals are not privileged. After this greeting, the moon looks down at me again.

"In this story, the value of the ring appears to wax at certain times and wane at others. But true value really lies in the heart of the beholder, not in the price or even the rarity of a thing." He smiles expressively at me as moonbeams slowly drip like tears from his eyes. "People," he continued, " are something like that ring: every individual has worth. The key is to find another person who values the worth you possess. Then you will have infinite value."

Chapter
Seven

A waning Light

As I sit on the porch, I hear the faint sounds of some neighboring amateur pianist. The music stops abruptly with each mistake, and when it begins again, it's not very soothing, yet the muffled tones are inspiring.

"I sometimes think I should enjoy learning to play the piano," I remark casually to the moon, who has been staring at me for some time now. He appears to be in a thoughtful mood this evening. "If you could play any musical instrument, which one would you choose?" I ask him. His expression becomes solemn as he considers the question. He blinks once, and then I watch some celestial breeze tousle his goatee. He immediately straightens it through intense concentration. Then he relaxes his expression again as he reflects on the question.

"I am too complex," he responds in a most serious

and somewhat patronizing tone. "There is no one instrument that would be adequate for me to express myself completely. It would take several instruments. An entire symphony, perhaps."

"Ah. You are a vocalist. I should have known."

"A vocalist?" He begins to laugh at the idea. The laugh is slightly pompous, but it connotes his genuine amusement at the idea. "A singer does not play an instrument."

"Yes. But what's a song without words? When a vocalist sings, he draws attention to himself. He has the one thing that no instrument in the entire orchestra has: words. He has more than melody, harmony or rhythm. He has a vocabulary and the rapt attention of the audience -- just as you convey a light to earth that is unique and you provide an ambiance unlike any other."

"Yes. I contrive a rapt attention every night," he agrees with solemnity. Then he winks, and I watch moonbeams flood from his eye as it reopens. The sudden downpour is brilliant but does not hide his facetiousness. "Perhaps I shall sing for you."

"Tell me a story, instead," I plead. Of his singing I knew little. His stories I already knew were wonderful.

Heraclitus said that you can never step into the same river twice. The flow of water continually moves and carries so many objects in each current that the river is constantly in motion and changing. Clouds are never the same, either. They're formed by the personality of the water source from which they're made, but then they maintain a separate motion all their own. Clouds are original. A cloud's water may come from a river that's constantly changing, but the cloud is of a different nature altogether. It is independent. And while rivers are tangible, clouds are ethereal. Most people walk along the banks of rivers and dream among the clouds. Joe was different.

Joe grew up by the Ohio River, but Joe and the river were made of different stuff. No matter what phase the river was in, Joe's life took the opposite course.

For example, when the river was a torrent, things were peaceful for Joe. When the river was calm, Joe's circumstance took the sudden and rapid turns of a weather system churning a vortex of wind. Whatever the river did, the situations in Joe's life did the reverse. Joe was more like the clouds that were formed of the river's essence.

Joe was an extraordinary musician. His talent was more than genetic ability or training, although he practiced constantly. It was as if an angel kissed Joe's fingers at birth and imparted them with remarkable agility. While the visual spectacle of his playing was a blur of activity, the sounds were clean; the tones full and pure. He knew music better than he knew any person, and he walked the plains of rhythm and harmonization the way that most of us fall into a dream. He slipped easily onto that plain, and then he went wherever it would take him. Music was his natural language: the language of heaven, and he spoke it with fluency. When he played, everything seemed a little more beautiful. It was as if a supernatural voice whispered the secret of melody into his hands and breathed the mystery of harmony into his soul. But just as the content of a river fluctuates with time, the situations in Joe's life constantly moved between harmony and dissonance.

The February when Joe was born was unusually cold and dry, but the Ohio flowed strongly and supplied water for all the animals flocking to her banks. Life did not come to Joe as easily as it flowed in and around the river. Joe was hospitalized immediately after birth for a heart condition. The doctors were concerned that he would never make it past his second birthday, but he did. He was a frail but good-natured child who smiled at everyone. He must have been stronger than they suspected, because Joe astounded the doctors repeatedly. He recovered from numerous illnesses during his early years, and his heart grew a little stronger with each birthday.

When Joe was about seven years old, his father, Douglas, attempted to take Joe down to the river. Douglas thought the river air would be healthy for Joe. Douglas tried teaching his boy to swim in an effort to strengthen Joe's muscles and frail looking limbs.

"Kick harder!" Douglas screamed. "Show the water who's boss!" Joe's legs flailed wildly but imprecisely for more than an hour. The next day Joe caught pneumonia and spent most of that summer in bed. The following year Douglas took Joe fishing, but Joe was too motion-sick to sit in a boat. Joe could barely hear Douglas talking with the land swirling around him, making him dizzy. When Joe emptied his stomach Douglas told Joe that he would get over the sickness, but he didn't. He vomited so much that he became dehydrated and had to spend the night in the hospital.

Douglas then decided to try fishing from the bank. But Joe's boot became stuck in the muddy soil along the edge. The gooey earth suctioned the boot firmly into place and then rotated Joe's ankle so that as he was trying to free his trapped foot, Joe slipped into the river, spraining both of his ankles in the fall.

"You're a fish outta water when you're in the water," Douglas observed as he helped Joe onto the bank and back home. After that day, he relented and left Joe alone.

Since Joe couldn't run up and down the banks of the river like other children, Grandpa gave Joe a guitar as a birthday present. Joe practiced several times a day, and as his fingers strengthened, so did his heart. It was better than medicine. By the time Joe reached his teenage years, he was as healthy and rebellious as any other child.

During the winter that Joe turned fifteen, there were several heavy snowfalls. When the accumulation melted, the river began to swell to the fullest it had been in years. The water engulfed low layers of vegetation and tore younger plants from their resting places within the banks. As the river rose to its crest, so did the frustration within Joe's father.

Douglas started pushing Joe to stop playing the guitar and start thinking about a trade. Music was a frivolity to Douglas, and he didn't understand why Joe would waste most of his time practicing. When Joe was younger, Douglas never envisioned Joe would live long enough to have an occupation. Now that Joe was getting older, Douglas became concerned that his son would never be able to support a family on a career that, to him, seemed nothing more than a whim.

"One day you'll have to wake up and earn a living like the rest of us," Douglas continually admonished Joe.

"I will earn a living. But not your way," Joe insisted in his typically quiet but firm manner. Joe smiled in a genial, self-assured manner as he pushed his growing hair out of his vibrant green eyes, but Douglas turned away in anger. Douglas was a working-class man who understood only the role of a man as the family provider. While other people saw Joe's talent, Douglas saw Joe as only an impudent boy who didn't know how to fish.

It was Robert Frost who said, "You don't have to deserve your mother's love. You have to deserve your father's. He's more particular." Douglas was one of the most particular fathers. He challenged Joe often. He felt it was his duty to prepare his son for life. Music wasn't real to Douglas, and there was nothing more real to Joe. Because of this, Joe didn't respond to Douglas's coaxing, and Douglas became more and more concerned for Joe's future. Douglas pushed. Joe pushed back. Tempers continually flared and popped with a bang, like an old roadster backfiring as the engine turned. Then Douglas decided to get tougher on Joe. When Joe went to church in high tops and jeans, he was told to dress more respectably or stay home. He chose to stay home.

Whenever Douglas told his son not to do something, Joe broke out of his usual calm and reflective nature and went out of his way to prove that he could and would do it. Douglas could not believe that the frail child whom no one expected to live more than two years could be so obstinate. That summer as the Ohio peacefully flowed with contentment, Joe's life raged with conflict.

"Cut your hair or find a new home," was the ultimatum that Douglas finally offered. Joe did the only thing that he could do: he left home and went to live with his older sister, who was now married. Douglas refused to speak with Joe, and Joe made no effort to see his father. As the Ohio moved into a rapid pace that autumn, Joe settled into life with his sister, her husband and their son. Joe helped out around the house when the school day ended and continued to practice the guitar at night. Life was busy for Joe, but late at night he was left alone with his music, and it was a time of healing for him. He lined the crack at the bottom of his bedroom door with pillows to muffle the sound and practiced in his room long after the rest of the house was asleep.

During his senior year Joe won first prize in the high school talent show. After graduation he kissed his sister goodbye and drove to Nashville, breathing in the summer dust through open car windows and feeling the hot wind in his long hair. At first Joe worked odd jobs to help pay his rent. He loaded blackened trucks with boxes of bright colored fruit as he sweated in the early morning sun. He delivered flowers for a stylish florist in the West End area but quickly gave up that job when one of the other boys made a pass at him. With a slightly mechanical inclination, he managed to find a job selling parts for industrial heating and cooling units. In the evenings and on weekends, he took any job he could find playing the guitar. After a few years had passed, he started selling his own songs. As he put in time on the less desirable jobs in music, Joe began to earn the respect of more established artists and then started playing on recording sessions. Within a few months he went on tour with some of the biggest names in the industry. He was never unemployed, and he constantly worked to enhance his playing.

Joe's career thrived. The first few songs that he recorded on his own caused a big stir in his hometown whenever they aired on the radio. The only person not talking about Joe during this time was his father, Douglas, who refused to acknowledge Joe's career or existence. Douglas talked less or stopped talking entirely whenever Joe was brought up in conversation. He tried to appear diplomatic by saying nothing, but everyone saw the tightness in the way he held his mouth. Once Douglas clamped down on his teeth so hard, he bit the cigarette he was smoking in two, the lighted half plunging to earth like a fallen star.

Douglas spit out the remaining fragment and walked away silently, both of his hands tucked away in his pockets like a shy child.

During the time that Joe started gaining recognition in the music industry, the water level in the Ohio began to drop. At first the decrease was slight, and hardly anyone noticed it. After two years of low water, people began to notice, and officials began to investigate. The river continued to dry up for another year, withholding the causes in secret where no one could diagnose or help it recover. The Army Corps of Engineers was baffled by it. They studied the river and researched the history, but the reason for the low water was a mystery. It didn't make sense. There was abundant rain but never quite enough to fill the wide expanse between the banks. People joked about being able to walk from one side to the other if the water got much lower. Then there was a chemical accident. If the water had been higher, perhaps it would have quickly washed the poison away or diluted the effects. All forms of life along the edge of the river suffered. Fish and vegetation died, leaving a stench as the rotting mess drifted on the low waters. Many people decided that the river would never recover as it struggled to regain ecological balance. But like fate, rivers are strong. The Ohio was dwindling but would not die out. Rivers enjoy having the last word, and they usually do.

As Joe continued to be successful, he wrote songs about the river, about his home and about his grandfather, who taught him to play the guitar. It was the song about his grandfather that won the Grammy award, and Joe played the song on television. To hear Joe's music, one would never have guessed that his relationship with his father was strained. When Joe played music, it was as if all the ugly things in life fell away and only the beautiful things remained. Perhaps they did for Joe, who had started a family of his own. He loved his children unconditionally and made time for them no matter how busy his schedule became. Joe loved to talk about his kids, but whenever people asked about Joe's childhood, he would answer, "I learned a lot as a child. The most important thing that my parents taught me is that not everyone is the same."

As the years passed, it was clear to everyone that Joe's success wasn't a fluke. After more than a decade, Douglas wouldn't admit he was wrong for trying to steer Joe away from music. A few times Joe's mother tried to get Joe and

Douglas to speak to each other again, but neither Joe nor Douglas would succumb.

"Douglas," she begged one hot Sunday afternoon, "a lot of time has passed, and what it looks like to me is that the two of you won't forgive each other for being too different from one another. Well, I can see one way that you're both exactly the same. You're the two most stubborn men I have ever known."

"Stay out of it." It was the same thing Douglas said every time his wife brought up the subject.

"Well, the only thing sadder than the condition of the river right now is the way that you two won't talk." But Douglas still felt that Joe was wasting his life and that Joe's choice of career wasn't quite respectable.

"No good can come of this," Douglas said to himself over and over.

Although Joe came home to visit often, Douglas was unavoidably detained on business for every one of Joe's stays. Pride can have a very strong work ethic at times. Douglas didn't even show up to the benefit concert where Joe played in order to raise the money needed to clean the river.

"If everyone attending that event donated the same number of hours of hard work, we'd have the river cleaned up already," Douglas insisted.

"These aren't just local people attending. People are driving in from all over. People who don't care anything about the river are going to help us clean it because they want to see Joe. Joe cares enough about the river to make this happen. I just can't believe that you don't care enough about Joe to be there for him." Joe's mother was in tears for days over the issue.

"Joe doesn't need us. He has thousands of people who are going to be there for him." But when everyone else was gone, Douglas turned on the television and watched Joe from the comfort of his own home, where no one else could see him and he didn't have to swallow his pride. Douglas watched closely, and for the first time he listened to the words that Joe sang with feeling. Douglas watched his son's dark wavy hair as the wind gently tossed the strands around his face, sometimes leaning into his empathic eyes. When he played the guitar, he'd tilt his head to one side, usually the left. Douglas noticed things about Joe that he'd never perceived before, like the way Joe seemed more relaxed with a guitar in his hands. Joe also had a particular way of smiling halfway when he knew that there was something funny, or just nothing to really worry about. Halfway through the concert Douglas suddenly snapped the television set off. "He never could fish," Douglas remarked to himself, as he picked up the loosely folded morning newspaper, which he'd thoroughly read earlier. He was asleep long before his wife came home and woke up only briefly to acknowledge her return. She knew enough not to tell him about the concert, so she told him about the traffic instead.

It was only a few weeks later that Joe's grandfather died. When Joe and his father met at the funeral there was a brief and formal exchange of conversation, as if they had never met before. Then they avoided each other's company until the funeral procession began and both of them were called to assist in bearing the casket.

They walked silently, stoically next to one another for a short bit, but it seemed to Douglas that Joe wasn't carrying his share of the weight, and he couldn't help quietly mentioning this fact.

"I guess that when a person gets too successful, they're

not used to hard work like the rest of us." Douglas was sorry as soon as the words came out of his mouth but held his chin up as he waited for Joe's reaction. Joe smiled in his usual easygoing manner but didn't speak.

What Douglas didn't know is that Joe already had terminal cancer, and Joe had not told anyone but those who were closest to him. He had not even told his own mother because he knew that she couldn't keep a secret from Douglas. Joe despised grandiose and false sympathies, and so he avoided them to the end.

"People who didn't care to be around me when I was alive certainly don't need to be standing here, watching me dying," Joe told his sister as she sat on the edge of Joe's bed a few days before he died. "It's easy to love someone who isn't going to be around. Right now I need the people who loved me while I was here on this earth. I'm not complaining, Sis. I've had a great life. I have you, and I have my wife and kids. You've all been the best things in my life. Nothing can replace the love of your family. But your family is the people who stick around and love you for who you are. I know that Dad wasn't perfect. Neither was I. But when you're family, you support one another, even when you don't agree. We had a lifetime to work out our differences, and it didn't happen. Now that lifetime is over."

The next time Douglas saw Joe was at Joe's funeral, and Douglas saw his son very differently. It wasn't the way that Joe's long curls were arranged neatly around his soft face or the way that his arms were gently folded. Douglas suddenly started thinking that all the small things didn't matter anymore. It's odd how the size of things that matter can decrease with time. As pride and stubbornness atrophy into rich compost, better things are given the freedom to grow there. Joe was gone, and now Douglas thought about things that were more important than the length of a man's hair or how well someone could fish -- things like how he loved the way that Joe threw a baseball or how much he enjoyed his grandchildren.

The day of Joe's funeral, the river overflowed her banks and spilled into the streets of nearby towns without inhibition. Nothing held her to her course, and her destination was wherever she chose. Thanks to the money Joe raised during the benefit concert, the water was pure again, perhaps cleaner than it had ever been.

Like the river, Douglas was overflowing with

thoughts and emotions he never imagined he could feel. There was so much in Douglas that was left unsaid. The light of Joe's young life had waned. But the light of his father's love was reaching its fullest phase. This unfortunate man finally learned how to love when he had his son no more.

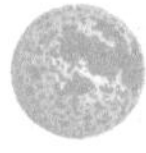

"I spend a great deal of my time watching the clouds. They fascinate me," the moon explains. He pauses to wink impishly at a nearby star. "The clouds of water vapor that cover the surface of the earth are like the clouds of time. Neither can be captured or held for very long, and both were designed to be in motion. We can admire a beautiful sky or a wonderful moment, but neither lasts one instant longer than necessary." I sigh as I breathe in the warm, grassy scent of a summer breeze. I know that this moment is almost finished, but I will bathe in the embers of his light as long as the moment lasts.

Epilogue
Concluding Remarks

I've learned a great deal from the moon. We're the closest of friends, and our lives are intertwined. When I look over my past, I see that the stages in my life are like the phases of the moon. I've had periods where I was the waxing gibbous: fat with wealth and success. There have been other seasons when my happiness was like the waning crescent and I watched my joy fade away slowly, merging with the atmosphere around me as if it never existed. Then I felt as if I was left with nothing more than an illusion, but happiness returns in time and glows once more in corpulent fullness. It's time that makes the difference. Or perhaps it is my perspective on happiness that determines how much of it I see in my life. After all, the moon never really disappears, but there are times when we cannot see him because of our own position in relation to him, as well as to the sun.

But the sun is another story, and that would take up too much space to include here, even if the moon tells it particularly well.

By this time you may believe me, or you might be skeptical that the moon really told me all of these things. Perhaps he has spoken to you, and you know him, as well. Or perhaps you think that my conversations with the moon are all in my head. It doesn't matter. If the moon should seek your attention, you will give it to him.

Also available form Fields of Gold Publishing, Inc.

He is Born

A Christmas instrumental recording.

Go to

www.FOGINC.com

for more information.

For information on new titles and recordings, please

check our web site periodically.